Praise for *The Waterb...*

"*Your book is wonderful. I was fascinated from...* When I got to the Medieglot, I was enthralled. Bu. ...hen I saw where you were headed with Richard and Michael, I was in awe.*"

  – Jan Price, Quartus Foundation

"*Although the book has many layers of meaning, and although its depths will be fully understood only by those who have journeyed as deeply as Repath has, his skill as a storyteller and the eloquent simplicity of his language will attract many readers. Others will immediately recognize it as a meditative work to be pondered and treasured, page by page.*"

  – Donald Evans, author, **Spirituality and Human Nature**

"*This intriguing tale of the future offers a possible solution to the chaos and fear of our present times. Although leaving the choice up to us, the author, a unique visionary, challenges us all to become waterbearers.*" – Morgana & Merlin, House of Avalon, England

"The Waterbearer *is a rich harvest of wisdom, especially for our times; it is an arrow of hope to guide us into the future and to welcome courageously the new millennium.*"

  – Jim Conlon, author of **Earth Story, Sacred Story**;
    Director: Institute in Culture and Creation Spirituality

"*For both of us, this book was an experience of the power of mature love to redeem all that it embraces. Told in stunningly, beautiful and evocative images,* The Waterbearer *refreshes the thirst of heart, soul and senses. This engaging book will continue to give gifts of new layers of meaning through many, many readings.*"

  – Dr. Janice Brewi & Dr. Anne Brennan, authors of
    Celebrate Mid-Life; Founders of Mid-Life Directions

THE WATERBEARER

Austin Repath

Reed Press

ISBN 0-9697399-0-7

Edited by Louise Hooley
Cover by John Zehethofer

First Printing

Canadian Cataloguing in Publication Data

Repath, Austin, 1935–
   The Waterbearer

ISBN 0-9697399-0-7

I. Title.

PS8585.E63W3   1994 C813'.54   C93-094798-3
PR9199.3.R46W3   1994

Now I saw a great sign appear

in the heavens, a woman adorned

with the sun, standing on the moon.

Her time had come and she cried

aloud with the joy of birthing.

Then another sign appeared in the sky:

a huge dragon, flaming red,

with seven heads. His tail

swept a third of the stars from

the heavens and spilt their riches

across the earth.

From
REVELATION 12:1,3

Chapter One

"Greetings! You are on the eve of your great evolutionary leap! Long have you struggled in darkness and ignorance – and long have we marveled at your courage over terrible odds. You have at last arrived at your most glorious moment.

"Now you must move forward. But you must take great care in this, your initiation. You are more vulnerable than you have ever been in all the long years of your earth evolution."

Richard slipped out of his terry-cloth robe and hung it over the hook on the bathroom door. Shivering in the cool air, he hugged himself for a moment. Then he stepped into the shower. Under the deluge of hot water, his muscles began to unclench.

"You are now within the final working out of human destiny. Either you will evolve to a new plane of consciousness, bringing the planet with you into conscious life – or you will pass away into nothingness, leaving it inert dust. Whichever way you choose, the risks are real and terrifying. Your species is on the brink. The urgency of your plight is overwhelming."

The shower was indeed relaxing. His favorite pastime: standing under a fountain of running water. Richard sighed deeply.

When he'd finally dared mention this voice to his analyst last week, Hornyng had been surprisingly reassuring. People under pressure often hear voices, Hornyng had said. Richard was certainly under pressure. His job, his relationship, even perhaps his sanity – all of them seemed on the line these days. And it was not just his own life that looked to be in crisis. His girlfriend, Pam; his best friend, Malcolm; even perhaps Hornyng himself – each seemed gripped in a similar kind of breakdown. Could a person catch a breakdown from somebody else? Richard wondered.

"But though the urgency of your plight is overwhelming, though never before in all earth's history has so much depended on the choice of a single generation – within the plan, all is as it should be. Your species' moment of awakening is at hand.

"If you can brave the trials, the potential outcome staggers even our vision of the possible. Within your lifetime, you could see the birth of all you dream of: your earth shining in the cosmos, a luminous pearl; your children, a race of star people, first-born of all the cosmos. And though you stand unaware, every fiber of the planet is at this moment calling you forward into this new dimension. Whether you choose to win through to godhood or to fall back into the void, we, your guardians, stand at your service."

Richard had thought a shower might still, or maybe dull, the voice. In a further attempt to unlock his muscles, he rolled his head in slow circles under the water. At least Hornyng had given him a new perspective on his situation. "There's nothing to worry about in hearing a voice," he had said. "Danger only arises if you try to deny the voice is there."

Richard had marveled at Hornyng's percipience. How many times in the past weeks had he tried to make this voice go away? He'd only worked himself into a state of breathless terror. At the end of the session, Hornyng had made a curious suggestion. His analyst had been holding open the door after their three-thirty appointment. As Richard stepped through it, he'd commented: "If all else fails, you might try talking to the voice. After all, you might have things to say to each other."

Of course, Hornyng's suggestion was absurd. Richard had no intention of chatting with a figment of his imagination. It could talk forever if it wanted to. He had too many other things to worry about.

He slipped out of the shower, grabbed an enormous bath towel and padded across the hall into his study. He looked down at the model sailing ship he was building. It was almost finished. And what a beauty! He'd molded the hull out of clay and had finished it with a special glaze. The rigging and cabin were all in place.

He tucked the bath towel around his waist and sat on the blue broadloom carpet. He'd patterned the boat on a late-nineteenth-century sailing vessel, modifying it to fit his purposes. It looked finished, but it needed something more. He'd been wondering if it really needed a bowsprit. In his head, the voice resumed as though it had been waiting for an opening.

"In service to your race, I have been sent to present you with a task. I am here to put before you a more extreme version of the present situation so that you will be able to see present reality more clearly. Thus, brought face-to-face with the forces now in existence, the particular way you choose to deal with this challenge will determine your species' future."

Richard sighed. Whether he could find a way to live with the voice or not, he had to give it full marks for persistence. From that first word, *Greetings,* to this stuff about a task, he'd been hearing the same message repeated for…well, for how long? It was one thing to be hearing a voice in his head. It was quite another to have heard the same voice saying the same words so many times he could probably, given a try, quote the whole thing verbatim. If he were actually to take Hornyng's ridiculous advice, his first thought would be to wonder whether all this stuff were, in fact, even imaginary. Maybe it was a real transmission. Maybe this same message was being beamed to every person on the planet. Most people would brush it off, regarding it as evidence only of a neurotic mind. But if one didn't brush it off – what then?

He put the model down and studied it.

"Greetings!" the voice began again.

How many more repeats could he bear? Richard broke in. "You talk of a world more real than our own. What, pray tell, might this scenario look like?"

To his surprise, the voice answered his question. "The Middle East is the center of a conflagration so devastating that the whole Mediterranean basin is destroyed: Jerusalem, Mecca, Athens, Rome. The source of all the major Western religions, of all Western civilization, is obliterated."

"This could happen?"

"It will happen. Unless your race chooses to take a different course."

"What does this have to do with me?"

"Enter this possible plane, an extrapolation of today's reality. On this plane, you could change everything. On this plane, you could find the source of new life. Life, awaiting your hand, your skill as a carver in wood, a molder of clay. Life, waiting for you to create a form fitting for a new humankind. On this plane, you could carve out a new image of man."

"But..."

"Of course you are unsure. You feel the task too large, yourself not able. You feel you would betray yourself, and by betraying yourself, betray all the world, for all time. Yet have faith. Great forces have been put at your disposal. I myself have prepared a place for your healing."

"Who are you?" Richard demanded.

"My name is not unknown to you. Nor is my image. When the time is ripe, you will know more fully who I am."

The phone was ringing. Richard ran to pick it up.

It was Pam. "You promised you wouldn't be late! I'm waiting for you!"

He had promised to be at the New Year's Eve party she was holding before midnight. "I'm just leaving," he lied.

He put down the telephone, feeling guilty. Life with Pam had been difficult lately. A year ago, with his encouragement, his girlfriend had turned her love of partying into a small business, Fun Galore. At first, she'd seen providing an evening of corporate conferencing with a little fun as a challenge. But lately, as Fun Galore prospered and the number of engagements grew, she'd been finding the task of providing gaiety an increasing strain.

He knew she'd make a scene if he didn't show up before midnight. But then, what was their life together these days if not a succession of terrible scenes? Richard had never thought it necessary to tell Pam that he abhorred these affairs. But how many more of them was he going to have to live through? He loved her and cared for her, but it was getting harder to deny his doubts about their relationship.

At least when he was with her, the voice went away. He paused and listened. Silence. He had to give her that credit: her call had rescued him from that disturbing dialogue. For this, he felt a wave of gratitude. "I mustn't be late," he muttered.

He sat down again on the plush carpet amid the clutter of his model building, picked up the vessel and looked along its length. It wouldn't be easy to join a wooden bowsprit to a ceramic hull. He wondered which might work best, a glue or a resin.

Richard ran his hand over the smooth hull and imagined what it would be like full-size. He imagined himself in the tastefully decorated cockpit, the controls off to the side. He was at the helm, in control of the ship.

"You have done an excellent job of designing her, Richard." The voice was back.

"Thank you," Richard responded in mock seriousness.

"Have the steering controls been checked?"

"They have checked out well beyond my specifications," Richard replied. "Now all I need is a destination."

"You have a destination," the voice insisted. "You have to chose to heal the warring factions within your being. Humankind is on the verge of destroying the whole planetary organism. The urgency is overwhelming. You must choose to take on this task. It is your destiny."

"Oh Lord, not that again!" Richard spoke with irritation. "I've only one task to choose at the moment. Am I or am I not going to go to that New Year's Eve party? And if I don't get up and head off soon, I'm going to be in a lot of trouble!"

"You don't have much time," the voice agreed.

Richard nodded and looked at the clock.

"You don't have much time," the voice repeated. "You must move quickly. There is little time left."

Richard stood up, naked.

"The rewards of the journey will be well worth the risk. For it will take you beyond the despair of your race. It will offer you a way forward, where all that you dare not dream will be possible."

"Stop hectoring me. I need to get dressed." Richard reined in his mind, trying to still the voice by an effort of will. Yet the words continued. "There is much to be done." The voice had an urgency to it. "Time is short and there is much risk. Yet herein lies the glory of this millennium. If you can break free of the rule of opposites, if you can bring together madness and sanity, embrace both light and darkness..."

Anger swept over Richard. "For Christ's sake, lay off!"

"...The vessel stands ready, the womb prepared, the child chosen. But first, you must decide to undertake this crucial mission."

Richard wobbled under waves of panic. His mind felt loose. The voice went on, implacable.

"Energy beyond your wildest dreams has been put at your disposal. But you must make the choice. The future of mankind depends on you. You have not much time. You must choose. You must choose now."

"Go away!" Richard shouted, real panic in his own voice now.

The voice stopped, and he was left with his doubts.

What happened if all that the voice had been saying was true? What happened if, by his dismissing these words, he was indeed failing the entire human race?

He couldn't do what it asked. The voice was asking for too much. Fear of failing had haunted him all his life. Pam, his troubled friendship with Malcolm, his problematic job... He sat, paralyzed with the conviction that he was about to betray the whole human race.

The phone was ringing. He continued to sit, motionless. Two rings. Three. Four. Five. The phone went still.

"Trust her," said the voice. "She knows the way."

Silence.

Richard got up, started to dress.

Had he been dreaming it all? Yes, he must have been dreaming. He was shaking. He touched his face and found it damp with sweat. He had to get out. He walked around, picking out tie, shirt, jacket, pants. He dressed hurriedly, with a feeling of dread.

At the door, coat over his arm, car keys in hand, he caught sight of his model lying in the middle of the carpet. He put down his coat. When he picked up the model, he felt himself relax. "Mustn't leave you where anyone could find you," he said softly to the vessel.

He carried the model into his study, carefully slid back a wall panel revealing a large assortment of model vessels, all perfect and exact down to the smallest detail. He placed this latest one carefully inside. Looking at his tiny ships, he felt a sudden feeling of hope. No one knew about this side of him. It had been a secret kept since childhood. Not even Pam knew – only Malcolm. But that friendship looked to be over. Malcolm treated him as if he were an enemy these days. Richard sighed. Well. No time to worry about it now. Malcolm, too, had promised to be at the party. Perhaps tonight there would be time to figure out what had gone wrong between them.

The models were the most precious things he owned. He looked at the vessel one more time. Yes, he decided, it did need a bowsprit. He locked the wall panel, slammed his study door and headed out.

At the front door he stopped. In a spirit partly of daring, partly of defiance, he paused and yelled, "And if I don't choose to take on this task?"

Before him, slowly, a face appeared. It was fully three-dimensional, but without substance: a youthful face framed with grass-gold hair. The being was young, straight, tall – beautiful. Clear blue eyes looked out at Richard.

"No. Go away."

Another stepped forward to take his place, more youthful still. The promise of life shone from his brown eyes. Richard saw his child grown to manhood. His future looked out at him, asking.

"No, no. Go away!"

On they came, entering him, moving through him: men, women, children, infants, the offspring of a new race.

"Stop it," he cried. "Stop it. I can't do it. I can't do what you ask of me!"

But still they passed before him: the people of the future, radiant, loving, laughing. Their muted laugher rang through him. One after another they came, showing him the worth of his being, the light within his darkness. He watched the children of the future: the beautiful faces, the loving eyes. He watched as they came forward.

"Help me," he pleaded in the silence of his mind. "Help me. I don't want to destroy you."

Tears were wet on his cheeks. "Give me strength."

Then Pam appeared. She smiled. Her smile felt like it would pierce his heart.

"We will go forward together," she said.

He took a deep breath. He saw their children, looking up at him. He felt the pain of his love for them. He found himself speaking aloud: "I will not allow anything this beautiful to pass away into nothingness."

His voice grew to conviction. "I will not let it happen. I will do what you ask. Let it be as you see fit."

At that moment, the phone rang for the third time. He paused. Should he answer it or not? In a single decisive gesture, he reached forward, opened the door and stepped out into the center of the Maelstrom.

Pamela knew she was enjoying the mixer a little too much. It was unlike her. She excused herself by blaming it on the drinks Mel had been bringing her. A finger snapped somewhere; she realised there were five men waiting for her to say something.

"So, you give up?" she asked. "'To kick the bucket' meant to our ancestors what 'to take the next step' means now." She looked around at the five puzzled faces, her glance lingering on Mel. The computer controllers sprawled on a circular couch sunk into the floor area, listening while she held court.

Tobin sat back. "Tell us more," he said, smiling lazily.

"I could say I spent my time 'digging up' archaic expressions. That's a term from the times when people buried their dead. They never voided their bodies as we do here in Centrex." Pamela clapped her hands. "Here's one you'll never guess! What do you suppose 'your better half' is?"

"That's easy."

Pamela turned to the balding man sitting next to her on the circular couch.

"That's the half of Mel's life that he spends gazing down on the rest of the world."

"You mean while he's on the job, satellite scanning?" someone asked.

"You're wrong," Tobin announced. "It's the time he spends planning his affairs."

"Well, I know one thing. It certainly isn't the number of times he scores!" The balding man chuckled and the surrounding audience joined in.

"One moment!" Mel stepped into the center of the circle. "I feel like I'm being insulted. I don't see why I have to be subjected to your jealousies. Why don't you go find a good re-programmer and stay away from mixers until you can distin-guish your own problems from those of someone else?" Grinnng, Mel glanced around easily. He moved and spoke with the confidence of a man who knows he is good-looking. "Doesn't seem to me like I have problems." He chuckled and put his arm lightly around Pamela's waist.

Pamela's laugh had an angry edge. "Don't be too sure, Mel."

Mel laughed again. "Manners, young lady. Don't forget manners. They'll get you further than you might think."

Pamela suddenly caught sight of Richard at the bar, fixing himself a drink. At last he had arrived. She admired the way his clothes fitted, revealing his fine frame and accenting his shoulders. But she also felt the anger that had been brewing all evening. He was late again. And after all his promises!

She shouted across the room to him. "Richard, what is your better half?"

Richard had slipped in quietly as the two groups mixed. The room was the same as any other mixing room in the unit, and the mix followed the familiar format. Years ago, Centrex had decreed that the various work cycles should meet together socially from time to time to promote the interchange of ideas. This time it had been arranged that the scanners were to mix with the small group of transport experimenters working under Hornepayne.

"My better half?" Richard felt himself split in two. There before him in his mind's eye stood a child, its eyes clear, its face radiant. There before him stood his better half, a child of light. Then came cold eyes looking at him from hungry sockets, and the child was taken into the darkness. Richard felt like he'd lost his soul.

"Give up, Richard?" Mel's mocking words brought him back. He suddenly realized he was the center of attention.

"We're waiting for an answer." Pamela's voice echoed Mel's jeering tones.

"If this is another one of your quaint expressions, Pamela, I'm going to send you back to the twentieth century." For some reason, what he was saying sounded unreal to Richard; he could hear an edge of anger in his voice. However, before he could qualify his words, Mel had jumped in.

"But that, my dear Richard, is exactly what Centrex is paying you for. After all, you are the time-transport whiz. For all we know, you could have brought us all here. But you wouldn't do a thing like that, would you? Transport us all into a Centrex world, erase all memories of another reality and then play dumb, as if you didn't know anything about it?

No, Richard, you are too nice – too nice and too stupid – to do anything like that."

The whole mix laughed with Mel.

"And, by the way, I suppose things still aren't going well in the transport lab? But then, from what I hear, things haven't been going well there for some time now, have they?"

Before Richard could think of a suitable reply, Pamela rose and moved in front of Mel. "Has anyone ever told you you're an asshole, Mel?" She spoke quietly, her voice almost a whisper, yet her words were heard by everyone in the room.

Mel grinned back at her, unflappable. Nothing, it seemed, could perturb his poise.

Pamela turned and focused her attention on Richard. She stepped out of the sunken lounge and stood facing him, directly across the room. "Your better half – it's something any man would know in times when men practiced marriage."

Richard noticed she had dropped into Irish dialect.

"They didn't believe in hallucinogens or concubines or – " she paused and took a breath " – or even cohabitation. In those days a man and a woman came together and they loved in one flesh, and..." She paused, mimed the delivery of a child. "And they gave birth."

Richard met her eyes.

"If you lived in those days, Richard Cebornsky, you'd know well enough that your better half was the woman you married. She was the wife you loved all the days of your life."

There was some shuffling and frowning at her involving him in this public display.

Richard looked at this woman standing apart from everyone, facing him. Her eyes were flashing; her cheeks were flushed with emotion. She stood expectantly, awaiting his reply.

Richard felt speechless. This was a new Pamela, a Pamela he'd guessed at but had never seen before. It was as if a flame burnded up through her from some lost past – through generations of Irishwomen who had grown old trying to kindle their menfolk. For a moment, he remembered his earlier vision of a child wandering in a garden of warmth and tenderness. Then he noticed that everyone in the room was looking back and forth from him to Pamela, trying to watch both of them at once.

He wanted to joke, to pass it off, but he couldn't conceal his emotion. Pamela had publicly declared herself for him. He looked at the flame in her eyes, stepped away from the bar. Words started to form deep inside him – words he could barely trust, so long had he held them silent.

"Pamela – " he picked up his drink and raised it to her in what vaguely resembled the ancient custom of toasting " – I drink to that better half of you, the woman I see before me at this moment. I do in front of all present take you as *my* better half, as my wife, and promise to kindle thy empty womb and protect the child to come. This I vow, even if I have to cross to the farthest realms of possibility. So help me God." His voice was full and large, and seemed to come from a time beyond and thunder into the present.

Everyone turned.

Pamela stood, no longer defiant, but radiant. Richard had always thought her beautiful, but at this moment, her beauty had taken on an almost otherworldly quality. She was draped from shoulders to feet in a fine green fabric. Her long red hair tumbled, loose and glinting. She seemed not what she was – a recent arrival from Enclave Ireland, to be used for entertainment – but rather an ancient witch.

"And, Richard Cebornsky, I will be waiting for you when you return."

It was as if a spell had been cast across the room. Everyone stood, hushed and embarrassed at what they had witnessed. A declaration had been made between two people in their presence, and they felt the sealing of a bond stronger than the moment, larger than the space they occupied.

Finally someone clapped. "Great entertainment," Tobin called out.

Richard felt an urge to run across the room to Pamela and carry her off. But where in this artificial world could the life ritual be celebrated? He looked at his empty glass and decided to get a refill instead.

People formed into little groups to go over every detail of what had just transpired.

"They are indeed a strange couple."

"Really, she is quite beautiful, considering."

"They actually share the same quarters?"

"A little unusual, but then she is here as part of the entertainment roster."

"And she will be returned to her enclave."

"Richard Cebornsky is a little eccentric himself."

"No permanent harm done then."

The conversation was revitalised. The unexpected drama was channeled into words and dissipated, until the room was again bustling with pleasant social exchange.

Pamela looked across at Richard, watched him refill his drink. She wished he would come over. She looked around, but new groups had formed and no one seemed interested in her any longer. A nakedness she could not explain fell over her. She felt exposed and vulnerable.

Pamela looked around the room. She had indeed come up in the world. The people before her were some of the finest minds on the planet, all part of the select core known as computons. It was they who kept running the global computers in control of every aspect of human life. Without these men – she remembered how many times she had been told it as a little girl, back in Ireland – civilization would not exist.

She sighed quietly. Even with these people – the people at Centrex she knew best – she still felt like an outsider. But it was this quality – being different – that had gotten her north, out of Ireland. Sometimes she felt a little tired of being nothing but entertainment.

A voice beside her broke into her bubble. "I'd like to stand up to your better half."

She turned and saw a look of such obvious seductiveness on Mel's face that she burst into laughter.

"You mean you're asking me to dance?" she said, ignoring

the deeper implications.

"As you wish," he said smoothly, gliding her out onto the dance floor.

Richard watched Mel and Pamela dancing together across the room. He was never sure who he cared for more. Tall, blond, big-boned, Mel would stand out in any crowd. Pamela was shorter, but her auburn hair shone in the light and when she talked there was a quiet tenderness to her gestures.

Through Mel, Richard had come to know everyone on the grid. Mel had encouraged him to treat his professional life seriously. Together, they had advanced to high levels in the scanning field. The authorities had been pleased with them and had indicated that they would be favored if they went on to try for Green notation and the ultimate Scanner rating. Mel had gone on, but for some reason, Richard had held back. He'd ended up in what Mel still considered a backwater project – time-transport experimentation.

It was always Mel who came up with the great ideas – a trip to the new Sky Garden, a visit to the concubines or a gala appearance at the festivals that marked the year's passage. More than anyone Richard knew, he seemed happy. Mel acted as though all of Centrex existed only for the satisfaction of his own personal desires. Richard wished he could be as confident as his friend. Maybe Mel was his better half?

Richard reflected upon their troubled friendship. When had the problem started? It now seemed that every time he opposed or challenged Mel, he was the one supposedly mistaken. Richard smiled as he watched his friend maneuver Pamela about the dance floor. At first, Mel had been almost speechless with anger when he had learned that Richard and Pamela were sharing quarters. Eventually, as Richard had expected, he had come around. Richard watched as, across the room, Mel said something to Pamela. Pamela grinned and poked him affectionately in the ribs.

Richard felt badly about being late for the party. Pamela seemed to be acting as though he'd come late deliberately. It had been so long since he had talked to her about anything important. These days, her presence seemed simply to remind him of an intimacy he'd always longed for but had never been able to achieve.

From the corner of his eye, he saw a new figure coming toward him. Not Hornepayne! He sighed inwardly. What an evening this was turning into. First he'd been late for the party, then Pamela had been angry, then there had been that strange performance between them in full public view. Now Hornepayne! What did his boss want from him now?

Richard's first thought was to get away, but it was too late. The older man was coming straight toward him. Richard turned and smiled a greeting.

"Hello, Richard." Hornepayne put his hand on his shoulder. "Tell me, did the energy mazers equate positive in the LOMB sequence?"

"I'm in a time tunnel," Richard replied with mock seriousness.

Hornepayne seemed amused. "Don't worry, you'll get to the end of it."

Richard hated Hornepayne's cryptic comments.

Fortunately, he was saved from having to respond by the arrival of several others, who sat down and started to listen.

Richard looked up, hoping to catch Pamela's eye. She was still dancing with Mel, talking busily. Then he noticed Hornepayne eyeing him carefully. Richard snapped his attention back to the conversation around him.

One of the newcomers, a man who introduced himself as Omar, was scoffing at the idea his tutor had put forward, that the Mediterranean had been destroyed deliberately by the very countries that had thereafter established Centrex. "Have you ever heard of anything so preposterous?" he asked.

Hornepayne looked across to Richard. "Well, what were we told happened?"

Richard realized he didn't really know. "Why don't you tell us?" he suggested. "After all, you know the story better than any of us."

Hornepayne smiled and settled back onto the divan. "In the closing days of the twentieth century, as a finale to a century of mass violence and world war, a military black market arose in the former Russian republics. This missile trade could have been stopped – indeed, should have been stopped – but the economic temptations of such marketeering proved too great for these cash-starved economies.

"Thus, with far more ease than might be supposed, small rigid regimes and terrorist groups began stockpiling nuclear warheads, as well as a new kind of weapon – one advertised as being able to destroy whole populations without damaging roads, buildings or infrastructure. Of course, these new weapons had not been properly tested.

"Toward the end of the nineties, someone using these new weapons attacked Jerusalem, that city holy to three major religious faiths. Satellites initially reported the attack as a white light that flashed upward from the city. Then, as aftershock, flashes crackled outward across the Middle East and north across the Mediterranean. Northern Europe was protected only because of the Alpine ridge.

"The extent of the trauma is difficult for us to grasp. There were no rescue operations, for there was nothing to rescue. There were no retaliatory strikes, for there was no enemy to destroy: they had all been obliterated in the Maelstrom.

"The United Nations, as the convening governments of the time were called, met in round-the-clock sessions. No one knew what to do. Finally, the Security Council hammered out an agreement.

"Centrex was founded by world covenant. It was a product of fear, a measure taken to bring the unpredictable forces of worldwide nationalism under control. It's true that in declaring the area from the Mediterranean to the Gobi Desert a no-man's land, Centrex did, indeed, contribute to global calm. However, the ultimate outcome – Globe North, a tightly controlled administrative complex, and Globe South, a primary-industry region – did benefit northern interests, the very people, as your tutor quite rightly points out, suspected of fomenting the inferno, or as I prefer to call it, the Maelstrom, in the first place. And after the disaster, Centrex was built into the glacier ice of Greenland, from which they control the world."

"But Centrex had to impose global control," Omar interrupted. "The world was in ruins. A huge belt across the planet was filled with radioactive waste."

"Radioactive waste!" Hornepayne snorted. "What better excuse for the imposition of northern control over southern economic superiority?"

A younger man spoke up. "The north's walling off of the south certainly created an effective barrier."

"Yes. And why?" Hornepayne looked around at the group. "Many years before, people from globe south had already been accusing the north of working to place the planet under northern control. The Maelstrom provided the north with a perfect opportunity to bring this centuries-old political desire to fruition."

"Preposterous!" Omar exploded.

Hornepayne sighed, then said slowly, "Preposterous or not, it doesn't matter now. The only way we can change our present situation is by going back and changing past events so that the Maelstrom does not happen."

"But how will it all end?" Richard asked.

"One man needs to go and find out." Hornepayne looked directly at Richard. The mix fell into silence as the group waited for Richard to speak.

Pamela, sensing a problem, hurried over and jumped into the conversation. "Back in Enclave Ireland, we call that part of the world the Land of Cain."

"And who is this barbaric fellow you call Cain?" asked Mel.

"Well, you see," Pamela continued, "in Ireland, we still

believe in the Bible. It tells of two brothers, one called Cain, the other Abel."

"Sounds dreadfully dull," commented Mel.

"Only if killing your own brother strikes you as dull."

"Well, Pamela, my pearl of a girl, you're probably more right than you know." Hornepayne smiled at her in a knowing way. "This pattern we now find ourselves in can be seen in its simplest form as just that: brother killing brother. But with the help of men like Richard here, that pattern might well be changed."

Mel rolled his eyes and sighed audibly, but he watched intently as the old man put his hand on Richard's shoulder. Why, he wondered, did Hornepayne always favor Richard? Richard, as everyone knew, was a professional failure. It was he, Mel, who had won Green notation.

Pamela mimed a curtsy. Then she waved the group toward the lounge. "If everyone would join me where it's comfortable, I have a simulation game that I think you might enjoy."

Pearl of a girl. Pamela hated it when he called her that....

Hornepayne kept his hand on Richard's shoulder while the others filed away with Pamela. "Your journey is well begun – but only begun. Remember, Richard, we have faith in you." The old man smiled at him kindly.

"I think I'll go for a walk," Richard said. "There are things I must do."

"Go with God," Hornepayne said quietly.

Richard left the room without looking back.

Chapter Two

Richard wanted to be with Pamela – to touch her, caress her, smell her, consummate the pledge they had made. Instead, he found himself out in the open mezzanine of Centrex, across from the shaft of air, the mouth and respiratory system of the whole megaunit. Three-quarters of a million people circled this column of cold air built a mile deep into the glacier ice of Greenland.

He had left the party feeling as if he were about to explode. He ran and pressed his face to the portal glass of the air shaft. The cold against his cheek felt good, and he flattened his nose against the pane and made a face. He pulled back and looked at his reflection. The face he saw frozen in the glass was youthful, but seemed to be aching with an inner despair, like a soul caught in amber. He turned away from the glass. This was the part of himself he had no desire to see.

On the inner mezzanine, people were milling about, waiting for the buzz that would signal midnight and the start of another year. People pushed around him, pretending gaiety, yet their eyes were empty, their skin white and sagging like ghosts. They could all have been mannequins, their skin plastolax, their motions controlled by computer tapes. He watched a man celebrate the New Year by turning and walking into the Next Step. Richard shivered. He knew the minute the man closed the lead door behind him, a laser flash would disintegrate him. There were such booths on every mezzanine. No formality, no farewell, no grief. He felt the attraction of that solution.

He turned abruptly and pushed through the mob to the nearest elevator, and headed for the LOMB. He was greeted at the Laboratory for Orgone Mazer Bombardment by the electronic voice of the identifier. He cleared himself and the door slid open.

He headed for the control board, seated himself at the panel and looked out into the huge elliptical space where they did the bombarding. The room, if it could be called a room at all – it looked more like the inside of a giant chromium egg – was the largest unit in Centrex. It was a full 81 yards in length and 37 yards in width, a perfect ellipse of polished metal. At each end of the room, in the center of the two loci, were two small platforms. Any object on these platforms received the full impact of the mazer dischargers. After a while, the objects would begin to vibrate; left long enough, they disappeared. No one knew exactly where, but theory held that they were sent into another time dimension.

Richard pushed up the controls and watched the light beams as they cracked off the walls and intersected over the empty platforms. He thought back to the party and what Hornepayne had said about the horror of the Maelstrom. Had the North really done such a thing? It was unthinkable. Yet he could not deny the fact that something seemed to pervade Centrex like a deadly virus, feeding on the human psyche. Where would it end? He pulled himself back from such a question and focused on the problem at hand.

The challenge seemed simple. Richard had the theory and the formula to transport matter, even life-forms, out into time. However, as yet, he did not have the formula for bringing them back again. And, as Mel had rudely but accurately suggested at the mixer, it was at this point that he had been stuck for months....

Richard thought again of the way Pamela had publicly committed herself to him. Suddenly his mind reeled. And here he had been, hammering away at abstract mathematics for months! In some crazy way the voice had been right: woman did hold the key. The Fourth Coordinate was, to use one of Pamela's quaint expressions, as plain as the nose on his face.

He thought of running to tell Hornepayne, but then paused. This might be too fanciful even for that open-minded old man. And yet Richard was perfectly satisfied with the solution. The only way to present it was as a proven fact. Suddenly he made his decision. He himself would risk going to the end.

Richard picked up the remote control, walked toward the nearest platform and positioned himself on it. He edged up the remote dials and felt the stimulation as the mazer beams danced off the reflecting surfaces.

He felt himself become lighter as every atom in his body started to vibrate. He pushed the controls to maximum and felt himself begin to shimmer with a delicate, almost pleasant sensation. Suddenly he was falling through space, as if the floor had vaporized. His head spun, his ears buzzed, a soundless wind rushed through his body. He felt himself falling over the brink of time.

Richard lay still, quivering in the feeble light of half consciousness. He felt as if he had been splattered across eons of time. His fingers scratched about for some familiar touch. Instead, his nails scraped through an ashy dust down to a hard rocklike substance. Every particle of his being spun in a desperate, frenetic dance. He waited for himself to settle, unwilling to open his eyes. Where was he?

Carefully, he cleared his eyes, removing the mucus that had encrusted his tear ducts. Slowly he forced open his eyes.

All about him was barren waste – rounded humps eroded by wind, once-molten layers of pinkish, almost flesh-colored rock. He looked at his hands. They were covered with ash. He tried to wipe them clean. He struggled to get to his feet. His head reeled and he fell back, scraping his elbow on the hardened lava. Where was he?

He looked around him, surveying his strange world. There was no sun, only empty space that hung dull and ochre overhead. The stillness sucked at him like a vacuum. He kicked at the ashen dust in an attempt to break the tomblike silence. He wiped his face with his hands. The strange beauty of this empty waste thrilled, even mesmerized him. He kicked again at the dust, watched it hang suspended, then slowly float down to cover him.

Suddenly the details fitted together. He had set the controls to future end time, then had turned up the remote to maximum.

"I've done it! I've done it!" His tongue felt dry and swollen when he spoke into the deadly silence. "I've transported." He jumped up and down. "Hornepayne, look at me! We've done it." He spun about in an awkward dance, tried to calm himself. He had set himself free.

He was now out of time. The next step would be to get back. For an instant he was chilled with doubt. How was he going to do that?

"The woman. Trust her," he heard a voice say.

Pamela came into his mind. Trust her?

"She is your hope for safe return," the voice repeated.

Deep inside, Richard knew the voice was right. But would Pamela care enough? Would she do her part?

"Of course she will," he told himself, trying to be brave.

Over to his right there seemed to be a low ridge. From the top, he would be able to see what lay about him. While he was here, he might as well explore.

Richard was nearing the ridge. He sneezed as the dust stirred about his feet. His breath caught in his throat. "Just a little farther," he told himself. For some reason, the sky seemed to be darkening.

Then he stood atop the ridge, held motionless by the sight of a strange columnlike structure off in the distance. It rose above the flat plain, the height of a mountain. It seemed about twice as high as it was wide. Its massive, dull gray form beckoned to him; it looked like a solitary tombstone.

For a time he stood, hands on hips, calculating the meaning of this shaft. There was life here, or had been. The structure stood so tall, so erect. What race of creatures could create such an imposing edifice?

He moved off the ridge, down across the flatland, feeling small and naked, like a mite crawling across a desert. He felt oddly absorbed by the structure. His eyes fastened on it. His mind raced ahead into its shadow, though it made him feel oddly alone and hopeless. He looked up. The sky was definitely darker.

He trekked on, lost in thought. What was it doing here, alone in the midst of such desolation? What would the edifice reveal to him?

Slowly, it came closer; it was over a mile high, nearly half a mile in diameter. He was caught in its lure, drawn toward it almost against his will. What a colossus! He whistled in disbelief.

At last he reached its base. His eyes followed it skyward. There were no doors, no openings, no hieroglyphics, nothing. It stood like a huge, hardened phallus.

He reached out and touched it: it was smooth as plastolax, the construction cement designed especially for the building of Centrex. This mile-high column of plastolax stood eloquently as death in the thickening darkness.

Richard slowly guessed the truth.

He sat down, his back against the monolith. This was Centrex. Or rather, what was left of it. That city of three quarters of a million people built into the Greenland glacier was now just an empty shell. What had happened? Where were his friends – Pamela, Hornepayne, Mel? He felt his sanity stretch beyond its limit, felt horror stir within him. Irrationally, he felt he was the cause of it all.

He forced himself back from hysteria to a point where he could still question; where he could keep his sanity – what little he had left.

Where was the glacier ice – that ice a mile thick that had encased Centrex? Where was the sun? There were not even stars in this sky. It was simply a void, a black hole in space.

It can't be! Richard thought. Everything – earth, sun, maybe even the universe – destroyed? His mind fought the evidence. He felt sick. Could it be possible?

There was no need to think further. It had happened. They had destroyed the whole planet, maybe even the whole system. He had come to the end itself.

He sat in the ash as the darkness gathered around him. Slowly the magnitude of the horror he was facing crept through his limbs. It had happened – the unthinkable.

He sat with his loneliness. He wondered how it had happened. He could not shake off the conviction that he had somehow been the cause. How had it been his fault? Had he failed some final test? He shivered as, by some strange trick of memory, he remembered vague words he'd heard somewhere, in a dream perhaps. Words about a task, about a special task for him. Though he searched his recollection for more details, all he kept hearing was – of all things – Mel's mocking laughter, ringing through his head.

He continued to sit. Had he failed to remember something and, as a result, had become the last man on earth? The thought numbed his mind. He felt the guilt, the unlived lives, the waste of time itself. Despair fell across his shoulders, heavy and motionless as wet clay.

He began to cry as he realized the truth. Everything was truly hopeless, over, finished. There was no way even to get back. He might as well just sit there and wait for death.

Only the aching of his heart told him he was still alive. In that ache there was hope. "The death of man does not happen without his consent." A voice seemed to come from a distant place.

"The death of man does not happen without his consent," Richard murmured.

"I don't want to die." His voice came to his ears, thin and shrill, sounding like that of a child. He could feel the warmth of his tears streaming down the ash on his face.

"Help me," he called out. Small and helpless, he sat there alone. "Help me out of this pit of darkness!" he cried aloud. "Help me!" The child of darkness reached out his hands.

Before him appeared a magnificent being. Richard stretched out his hands, watched as this shining creature lifted him up into his arms. He felt himself coming apart, starting to convulse. He was falling back into consciousness....

There was a buzzing in his ears; he opened his eyes. When he sat up he was in the control center of the LOMB.

The phone was ringing. It was Pamela calling him.

"I was worried when you left the party," she said. "So I called the LOMB. Are you okay?"

"I'm fine," Richard told her.

"You don't sound fine."

"I tell you I'm fine!" Why couldn't he tell her what had happened?

There was a silence from Pamela's end of the line.

"Don't worry. Please." He wanted to thank her, to have her hold him. But the words wouldn't come. "I'll tell you about it all later. I really don't have the energy to explain anything just now," he added lamely.

After another minute of silence, Pamela said, "'Bye, then."

Richard said goodbye and hung up the phone. Why had he not told her? He was grateful beyond belief that she had called him.

The wall clock showed that two hours had elapsed since he'd started the experiment. Slowly the realization dawned. He'd done it! He had traveled there – and back!

But when he stopped to think about it, he realised that, though he had solved one mystery, he had uncovered many more. Where had he gone? How, exactly, had he gotten back? A wave of nausea flooded his body. He had to talk to someone. He thought of Hornepayne, but he wasn't ready to see the old man yet. His relationship with Pamela was just too complicated right now.

Suddenly he thought of Mel. Mel was the only person at Centrex who might conceivably understand.

Mel opened the domlatch. When he saw Richard, he gave a slow smile. "Well, don't just stand there, come into my lair. So Hornepayne got to you last night?" his friend teased.

Richard sat on the couch and surveyed the room. He had always been intrigued by the collection of "toys," as Mel called them. The couch was covered by a real animal skin, a treasure smuggled from an enclave. A photostat of the sun rising over the glacier filled half a wall; Mel had had it framed to create the effect of a window looking out over a domain of Arctic ice.

His friend was bent over the sink, fixing a drink. His broad back was tense. It was odd, Richard reflected. Mel's back was always flexed to attack, yet his face was so relaxed and friendly.

Mel straightened and turned toward him. "You can't kid old Mel here, Richard. You came over to forget." He held out a steaming drink. "Here, this is just the thing."

"No thanks, Mel, I'm fine the way I am. Listen, I've got to talk to you. I've broken the time lock." Richard wondered how he must look to Mel, covered from head to toe with the ashes of a dead world. "Mel, you've got to listen. I've cracked it. The Fourth Coordinate – "

"The trouble with you, Richard, is that you don't relax enough. Have your drink. Then sit back and tell me all about your newest little problem in the LOMB." Mel switched on some music and lay back, waiting for Richard to drink.

He doesn't want to know, Richard thought. *He doesn't care.* Richard ran his hand through his hair. He had to make him see.

"Mel, it has to do with women..." he began.

Mel suddenly sat bolt upright. "Richard, you're a fool," he snapped. "You came here because you're upset at Pamela." His voice was biting. "If what you want is for someone to hold your hand and say, 'there, there, Richard,' don't come to me. I'm fed up with you coming here expecting support."

Richard spoke softly. "What I came to talk about has nothing to do with all that."

Mel's reply was bitter. "Are you so sure?"

He decided to try a different tack. "Mel, I've never seen you down. Why – "

"You know why?" he snapped. "I don't think about things. I don't let myself get down. It's that simple." He paused, then continued, "Richard, you're no fun anymore."

"Mel, what's wrong? For once, just for once, tell it like it is."

"You mean you don't know? Take that Cain and Abel nonsense, for instance. Cain got nothing. Abel got everything – even his father's blessing. Is that fair? You tell me. And if Cain can't get his share, he'll see that nobody gets anything. That's how it's going to be, Richard."

"But you have everything – top rating, prestige, position. You've got it all. What more do you want?"

Mel turned down the music and snarled at Richard. "Let me refresh your memory about a few facts of my existence. I was a test-tube baby. I didn't have a father to give me a 713 coding, like you. He was just sperm from the sperm bank. But I got myself an A49 rating after a lot of damned hard work. I'm listed as a global scanner, which puts me in a bracket well above yours – despite the fact that I live on the same grid as you." Mel pointed his finger accusingly at Richard. "But unlike you, I'm required simply to see."

"But you refuse to see anything."

"I see everything."

"You see only pictures on a video screen, Mel."

Mel didn't seem to hear him. "If there are dangers to crop production, I contact weather control. If there is unauthorized activity in the industrial zones, I contact worker control. But you know what? They do nothing. They just wait. Because in the end, it's always the same. The workers go on a little rampage, and then they go back to work." Mel pointed a finger at Richard. "But I'm not going to let it get to me. There's nothing that can be done. So I don't think about it. And you're not going to get me started."

Richard collapsed on the broadloom, staring. "Mel, you're not listening to a thing I'm saying." He got up and turned off the audio. "Listen to me. Just now in the LOMB, I transported to the world's end. And you know what? It's nothing but barren stone and ash."

"So what did you expect?" Mel said mockingly.

"What can we do? We have to do something. Maybe you and I could try – "

Mel backed away from Richard. "You can't change it." Then, noting Richard's expression, he added, "You seem surprised the world ends in destruction. But can't you see?

We're programmed to destroy. In the end, we'll destroy everything. It's the way we are. It's a curse. Rotten genes, bad seeds, an evil virus, the devil – whatever. Like it or not, Iscariot betrays, Cain kills. The world ends. Me? I just watch. Want some advice? Don't kid yourself. It's hopeless. So don't think about it."

Richard watched as Mel's eyes, at first angry, then for a brief moment imploring, grew dull and lifeless. He wanted to run toward his friend, put his arms around this man, breathe life back into him. But as he reached out a hand, Mel's anguish guttered and his eyes flashed arrogantly. Mel swallowed his misery and stood up, his muscles steeled.

"Get out!" he hissed. "Just get out. Now!"

Richard had no memory of bolting down the corridor. He felt like he was going to come apart, shatter into a thousand pieces.

Richard charged across the mezzanine, banging into people in his rush to get away. He saw a security officer move toward him. Quickly, he leaped into the nearest elevator, and found himself on a direct line to the roof. The Sky Garden was the last place he wanted to go.

What was happening to him? Everything seemed unreal, insubstantial, going in and out of focus. Was he losing his sanity? What had happened to Mel? What about world's end? No, he wouldn't let his mind go in that direction. What is real? he wondered. He realised he didn't know anymore. He must be imprisoned in a nightmare: that was the only conclusion his mind could come up with.

He stepped out of the elevator and into the Sky Garden – the only part of Centrex that was at surface level. He squinted until his eyes became used to the glare of the huge dome lamps that acted as sunlight. He walked slowly through the groomed garden of trees and flowers. Suddenly he realized that there was no breeze, no insects, no birds. It was just a bubble of nature protected from the Arctic night by an arch of plastolax. Though the plants were real, there was something lacking.

Suddenly he changed direction and ran toward the pressurized dome gate. He pushed down the domlatch, stepped through the antechamber and out into the frozen Arctic night. The cold air cleared his head. Here at last, he told himself, was the real world.

He looked up into the night sky. There he saw the group of seven stars that he remembered was named the Big Dipper. And then full remembrance of that day returned to him. It had been his seventh birthday, and his father had taken him here on their last visit together. How could he have forgotten?

"I must leave you soon." His father's words came back to him. "But there are things I must tell you before I go, things that will probably not make sense until you are ready to act. Listen carefully.

"The megaunit that you have lived in all your life was designed by me. Yes, I am the architect of this strange labyrinth. When you remember my words, it will be because you are seeing it for what it really is – a center of antilife, a point of control that perpetuates only an imitation of life. It was necessary that I build it: man had to externalize a vision of his hopelessness. The form could have taken flesh; it took instead the shape of man's own inverted genius. Behold Centrex.

"When you next remember my words, you will see that the world is indeed standing victim to its own 'final solution.' Yet all is as it should be, my son, for the architect always builds an exit. The means are at hand. Mankind has reached the point of no return. You must go forward. Do not lose hope, for the prize is worth the risk.

"For this, your seventh birthday, I would give you the seven stars of the Big Dipper. See how beautiful they are."

Richard saw again the constellation of the seven, heard again his father's voice. "There, waiting in the heavens, is a chalice of stars filled with undreamed-of riches. One day, you must reach up, take hold of the prize and pour its richness over the earth. This, my son, will be your reward."

Richard remembered how his father had picked him up, held him in his arms and then raised him up to the stars. Slowly the words came back to him: "One day you will awaken and look about you. You will see mankind burying itself alive. You must choose life, life for all of us. In your generation the choice will be made. But lest you forget, child of my wildest dreams, I give you a token of your destiny."

Richard reached up and felt hanging on a silver chain around his neck the small silver medallion of seven stars. He thought of his father's words. But how was he to accomplish what his father had told him he must do? He had seen the end, he had seen the despair, but he could not see beyond them. "Show me the way," he prayed.

The blackness of the polar night was illuminated by a faint shimmer. A voice came to him as from a far place. "Icharitas," it named him. "Icharitas." The voice filled his being. "Greetings. You are now ready to see as we see."

Before him, he could see taking shape a great orb, priceless beyond all imagining.

"See the earth as we do. Approach her in gentleness and love. Earth has been set aside for a special task. On her has fallen the forces harmful to the Solar Logos. She has taken them into her dense being, into her earth matter. Now her time of service is ending. Icharitas, your generation must call forth the darkness of the center – embrace it that it may be cleansed. With this act all things will be changed. Be not afraid. There are no words to describe the glory of what we see for you. For this moment was your race sent forth. Enter now into your travail. Go now into love. Learn. Then, deep in that realm of light, you will meet the test. Uplift the earth with joy!"

Across the wilderness of the polar night, Richard heard the sound of singing, faint and glad.

"Alleluia. Alleluia."

Pamela arrived home half expecting to find Richard, but there was no sign of him. She disposed of his dinner, then started to knit. She stroked the soft, furry wool and thought about their fierce lovemaking the night before.

When she'd finally come home from the New Year's Eve party, Richard had not been there. But shortly after she'd put herself to bed, he'd torn into their domitat, half weeping. When she'd asked him where he'd been, he'd seemed beside himself, babbling about a vision he'd had: about the end of the world, about an amazing being who had rescued him, about stars and singing. She had smiled at his desperate need to put everything into words, had put her fingers on his lips and had pulled him down on top of her. He'd given her everything he had in a strange impassioned mating that had brought her close to tears. Then, for some reason, he had gotten up, looked at her strangely and left the room. She remembered she had heard him open the door to his study. Then came a muffled, angry scream, and he had run out the door.

Pamela forced her mind to think about the video she was preparing on the ancient skill of knitting. She did not want to start thinking about where Richard could be. She looked down at her knitting, swore, and ripped out the last five rows. The needles clicked loudly as she began again.

It wasn't until quite late that Mel dropped over. She could tell by his face on the videophone that something was wrong. Mel sat in Richard's chair and stared at her. There was something in the way he looked at her, something in his eyes, that made her afraid.

"Pammie, he's left you."

"What do you mean?"

"He's disappeared."

"Well, don't look at me. It's not my fault."

"Did I say it was?" Mel asked, watching her. "You know Richard has been sending objects into transport. Well, it appears that on this occasion he's sent himself."

Pamela looked away from him. "You talked to Hornepayne?"

"He isn't sure what to do. He's waiting to see what happens." Mel paused. "Richard used to tell me how he'd put laboratory rats into transport. They'd disappear easily enough, but the only thing I know for sure is that nothing he's sent out has ever returned."

"All this stupid nonsense about rats," she interrupted. "Get to the point."

"Pam, did you and Richard have a fight?"

"We had a fight in bed," she said sharply. "Richard wanted sex but I didn't feel like it." This was a lie, but she didn't feel like telling Mel the truth. "He got mad at me and left."

She added as much as she dared. "I know he was upset, but you know how he is – he keeps everything inside. I expected the work in the LOMB would have settled him, the way it usually does, though he's been having troubles with it lately. I don't know what more to say." Why had he left her? It had been all right until he'd stepped briefly into his study. Then he'd seemed to go crazy.

"What is Hornepayne intending to do?" she inquired anxiously.

"If nothing happens, or if Richard doesn't show up in a day or two, he said he'd have to make an official report. But I doubt he will. Hornepayne knows more than he's letting on." Mel shifted position. "But what about you in all this?" he asked.

"I'm not sure," Pamela said hesitantly. "It seems like I'll have to move back into a single domitat."

Mel acknowledged her answer with a thin smile. "That won't be easy," he reminded her. "You're not the same girl you were when you met Richard."

She felt like she was, in some strange way, being tempted. He sat back with an easy nod, a wink that implied he'd look after things, that he wouldn't hold it against her.

"Look, Mel, I know what you're saying. But perhaps you don't know the truth about Richard and me. It's true I was just a bewildered girl from Enclave Ireland when I came north. But with Richard, I was no longer intimidated. He was my guide into this world. He could accept my confusion, my unsophisticated ways. You have no idea how good it felt to walk into a mixer with Richard. He gave me a confidence I'd never had before."

Mel looked sympathetic.

"Then we made a decision to cohabitate," she continued. "It seemed right that I move in. But something went wrong. I wasn't bored, exactly." She began to cry. "It was like I was programmed to switch off. Just when I was happy, just when a man loved me, I seemed to do have to do everything I could to hurt him, to push him away. I hated myself. And after a while, sex was different. I couldn't stand him touching me. I wanted him to go away, leave me alone. But that seemed to make him need me even more.

"I'll tell you something you probably won't believe," she went on. "Richard wanted me to hate him. I know it. He saw himself as a man no one could love. I tell you, we were destroying each other."

"The least you could have done was to leave him," Mel prompted.

"There were times I tried. But I couldn't. He would come in with a gift, headphones for the bibliotapes, for example. He knew I needed a new set. But I remember I simply threw them on a shelf and ignored them. So then he would go and lock himself in his study for the evening to do God knows what, while I would sit fuming because he was ignoring me. We were like vultures picking flesh off each other's bones."

Mel got up and went over to the headphones. He held them in his hands like sacred relics, looked across at her. "It was you, my dear," he said solemnly. "You sent the only man you loved out of your life."

She stood up to him stubbornly, fighting back her tears, believing his lie. "So what if I did? I'm glad he's gone!"

Mel looked angry. "Pamela, your heart is as warm as a stone!" He smiled at her nastily. "I don't know what Richard ever saw in you. I'd never partner with you. You're nothing but filth!"

"You're filth yourself," she spat back.

"At least I know it." He stood up to go. "But just remember – " he pointed an accusing finger at her " – it was you who sent him away."

Pamela laughed. "No, Mel, it was you. And we both know it."

Mel held the door handle and smiled maliciously. "Maybe you're right. Last night, before you two got home, I broke into Richard's study and smashed his precious little vessels. Oh, didn't you know about those?" he said mockingly. "Didn't you know what Richard was doing behind those study doors? Well, I smashed them good." He stood in the open doorway. "You're both crazy, do you know that? Crazy."

His eyes went cold as ice. He slammed the door behind him.

Pamela tried to walk off her unhappiness on the mezzanine, but she soon collapsed in one of the theme lounges. She sat before the video wall and watched as it gradually began to shimmer with sky, moon and stars. Slowly, she became absorbed by the slow movements of the projected heavens. She watched the almost-imperceptible shift of the stars, tried to identify the only constellations she knew, the Pleiades and Orion.

A waxing moon made itself visible over the edge of the screen. She felt a chill as she stared at its cold presence. There had always been something about the moon that offended her, even affronted her. It wasn't the source of its own light; it was merely a cold, orbiting sphere of frozen rock, reflecting back whatever shone upon it.

Suddenly she became aware of a computon on the couch beside her. He swung his leg idly, trying to catch her attention. She flushed with an anger she had almost forgotten. She was so fed up with these men. Everywhere she went, there they were. How dare he think she was a concubus? She got up, but the man rose and followed her. She tried to walk faster, but his footsteps kept up behind her. As soon as she turned the corner, she pulled open the emergency door. In the stairwell she leaned against the wall and listened to his footsteps. He searched for her farther down the corridor.

She started to walk down the stairwell, which ran three hundred stories from the surface of the Greenland glacier to bedrock. As she descended, she thought about the things that had brought her to Centrex. It had always been Centrex policy to keep people in the enclaves isolated. But her father had been a global citizen when he'd met her mother during his enclave-study module. Pamela had been insistent about her right to a global passport, but she had had to work hard to earn her way out of Ireland.

When she'd learned that Centrex had an entertainment unit, Info-Lux, which gave special privileges, she had prepared herself as an expert on the idioms and life-styles of ancient cultures. She'd sent off to Centrex her folio on pioneer wood furniture, and her notes on twentieth-century folk idioms she had done for her honorate at Dublin Convent College. And then one day, the summons came. She was awarded a global passport with a single word added at the bottom: *Conditional*.

Pamela had been more than pleased to leave Enclave Ireland, delighted to be stationed at the place her father had come from. But in the end, it had been a waste of time to have come to Centrex. She had wanted to find her father – or if not meet him, at least find out who he was. But the infoprobe would not release the records. You needed a surname, and he had never given his to her mother. She wondered where in this godforsaken place her father might be.

"Fool!" she shouted, to herself as much as to anyone else. "Damn fool!" She listened to her shout echo in the depths of the stairwell.

She resumed her trip downward. She remembered again the words of the Info-Lux evaluator who had turned up at a mixer the other night. "You should know that we'll be reviewing your Centrex contract shortly. It's conditional on the vogue for twentieth-century trivia, which as you've no doubt noticed has been waning." She remembered how she had shrugged. She was going out of style, but she didn't care anymore.

The sound of her feet on the stairs was almost hypnotic. On a whim, she decided to see if she could walk down to find the incubators. It was rumored that there was a floor deep in Centrex where the computons were genetically designed. She remembered a sliver of dream: herself as a beetle that split open to give birth. A silly dream, she told herself.

Suddenly she decided she wasn't interested in going any farther. On the next mezzanine level, she'd get out of the stairwell. But when she tried them, the doors were locked. She put her ear to the door. The hum of huge generators came back to her.

She thought again about Centrex birthing procedures. Damn them, she thought. That was slavery – using women to breed a race that, schooled and trained, governed in their turn. Yet amidst her anger, she felt a perverse fascination. Retarded slave women, used against their choice...Why should this idea fascinate her so much? She thought again about Dublin Convent College. Unlike the breeder women, she'd had a convent education.

At a lower level, she turned and tried the door again. This one was unlocked, but it opened onto blackness. All she could see was a red flashing light over the stairwell door and a recorded voice echoing in the darkness. "Power sources being adjusted. Temporary inconvenience." The smell suggested the whole section had been abandoned for some time. *Odd*, she thought, and continued her trek downward, not bothering to try any more doors.

Why had she bothered to come to Centrex, anyway? In the end, she'd only met Richard, and now, just like her father, he, too, had abandoned her. Suddenly she began to pound down the shaft. Her shoes on the metal frame filled the stairwell with echoes. Gradually her fury abated; eventually she was walking; finally, exhausted, she stopped. Only then did she become aware of the sound of footsteps rising from below. She waited until she could see who it was.

"Hornepayne! Where did you come from?"

"From down below."

"I know that..."

"Needed to get away from all that stuff out there." He gestured toward the curve of plastolax enclosing the stairwell. "Just took the tube down. Pressed the number that was my age. Got off about ten floors below us. My thoughts trouble me sometimes." He brightened. "But what about you? What are you doing here?"

"I was getting some exercise. I thought I might go down as far as the breeders. Not that they'd let me in, of course – but I've always been curious whether they existed."

"Oh, they exist." Hornepayne looked troubled. "Would you walk a ways with me, Pamela?" He smiled at her kindly. She looked at him. *He's old enough to be my father*, she thought as they began their slow ascent.

"The last while hasn't been easy for any of us, Pamela. I thought we had found a solution. Now I'm not so sure."

"What do you mean?"

"I'm worried about Richard." He looked at her broodingly, waiting for a reply.

It's almost as if he expects me to do something, Pamela thought. She didn't tell him that she wasn't sure she'd want to call Richard back even if she had the chance.

Hornepayne's voice broke into her thoughts. "Pamela, I've lost my faith in what we've been trying to do. I thought we could do it, but now I'm not so sure."

They climbed for a while in silence.

"And Mel worries me, too. I saw him coming out of the express tube last module. He moved like a man angry enough to kill anyone who got in his way. Yet the look in his eyes was of such pain. He didn't even see me."

Pamela decided not to mention her own scene with Mel.

"Something more is needed," he continued. "I keep getting a sense of it. But then it fades away."

Pamela gazed at him. This wasn't the Hornepayne she had seen before. Today he looked old, frail, transparent almost. She felt a sudden impulse to embrace him, hold him, reassure him, but she resisted the thought. She had nothing to give; her embrace left people cold. Then she surprised herself. "It didn't have to happen," she said abruptly.

"What?"

"That catastrophe in the Medieglot that you were going on about New Year's Eve. Maybe that's what's making you upset."

"Most people say it was the result of some horrendous accident," Hornepayne said. "What do you think?"

"I don't know. It seems like more than that."

"The war in heaven still goes on," said Hornepayne.

"You mean between Lucifer and the Archangel?"

"You know your Bible well, Pamela."

"I was educated in a convent school. But the nuns were like everyone else. They had no solution – they just repeated what they themselves had been told."

"But what if a way out could be found?" asked Hornepayne. "Maybe if Cain could have allowed himself to be touched, or if Lucifer…" He paused. "Or maybe it has to happen in each of us, or maybe in only a few. Maybe one would be enough."

Pamela spoke up. "There has to be something more."

"What do you see, Pamela?"

"A world where everything would be made new. Not just an end to the old enmities, not just swords into plowshares, but something that will make it all worthwhile. A new earth shining in the cosmos like a luminous pearl..." She broke off, feeling awkward.

Hornepayne turned to her and looked directly into her eyes. His voice dropped to a whisper. "'A woman adorned with the sun, standing on the moon – '"

"That's from the Bible," she interrupted. She tried to evade his gaze.

"From Revelations. Do you remember the next verse?"

The words rose in her mind: *...and she was pregnant, crying aloud in the joy of childbirth.* "No, I don't," she lied.

He kept looking at her. "You must accept that you, too, have been called forward."

Suddenly she heard herself shouting, "No! I won't!" She turned from him and ran up the stairwell. "I'm not a breeder!" Her feet pounded against the stairs. She felt angry beyond explanation or control. Her father had left her. Richard had left her. Once again, she was being used. And once again she would be discarded and abandoned. Never again would she be used, she vowed.

Never again.

Chapter Three

Richard looked about him, trying to get some sense of where he was. Behind him, he saw mountains, magnificent mountains that reached so high into the heavens they became lost in the blue of the sky. Far below him was open grassland, an expanse of golden grain that ran as far as his eyes could see. A flock of white birds flew over him, circled, looped and then as one dropped out of sight behind a nearby stand of pine. The sky was cloudless. Richard watched a green-and-yellow butterfly come to rest on a flower that bent almost double with its weight.

"Where am I?" he asked himself. Oak, pine, beech, fir – names floated up from memory. As he walked in the sunlight, smelled the vibrancy of living things, he remembered that the earth had once been covered with green forests.

He breathed in the sharp bright air, shouted out across the hills. He heard his voice echo his delight. Then he plucked a young fern, chewed it, savored the newness of growing things. A small animal climbed up on a rock and stared at him curiously. He laughed, called to it, but it scampered away.

His blood was bursting with life. To remain still was impossible. He began to run – long jumping strides, leaps that made him feel suspended in space. He ran until he could go no farther, until his body had spent itself of his bursting pleasure. He looked up at the sun, a bright golden orb that shone across the landscape. Richard felt its touch on his skin, in his bones; its sweet warmth softened the grayness of his being, the cold in his flesh. The sun stood directly overhead. He was shadowless.

Then, gradually, above the distractions of his body came a sound. Richard cocked his head, trying to make sense of this new thing. The sound was soft, enchanting. He followed it into the forest, let himself be drawn toward a small ravine. There he saw what he recognized as a spring, heard the gurgling rush of water as it fell from rocks into a shallow pool, green as emerald.

He stepped onto the soft moss of the glen, knelt beside the pool, drank deeply from the water, washed himself. Then he sat and leaned back against an oak, hands behind his head. He watched a small creek fall from the pool and wondered where it ended up. Some sort of enchantment had fallen over him. He lay back and dozed in the sweet air.

Richard awoke to the sound of birds. Slowly he rolled onto his elbow, trying to remember where he was. It seemed difficult to think.

He shook his head, rubbed his eyes. There, over by the spring, with a beam of sunlight illuminating his torso, stood the most beautiful being he had ever seen. The being bent over the pool and his long hair touched the water. Richard could hear him drinking. He was fascinated by the tanned arms, by the way the muscles flexed and rippled under the skin. Richard admired the grass-gold hair, the face. Their gazes met.

Time passed, both men gazing curiously at the other. It seemed they'd known each other since time began. Richard blinked.

The water rang again, leaves rustled in the wind. A man a little younger than himself stood across the water from him. Richard rose to his feet. "My name is..." He paused. A name echoed through his mind. It rang new to him, as if he had been newly christened, yet there was no doubt that it was now his name, just as there was no doubt of the rightness of this magnificent world, or of the being that stood there in front of him. "I'm called Icharitas."

"I'm called Michaal. Come, my friends are waiting."

Michaal led the way back to the clearing that overlooked the distant grasslands.

"David, Hospadar, Raheem, Sequitus." Michaal's voice rang through the forest. "He has come. Meet the ambassador from the north."

Somehow the title seemed correct, but Icharitas could not place the reason. He looked at the men who stepped forward to meet him. Each seemed so unique; each could have been a god.

He watched as they spread food on a fine cloth: fruit, nuts, bread, with rich golden liquids to drink. Michaal took the bread and broke pieces for them, offered Icharitas a strange oval-shaped fruit. Icharitas bit into it and felt sticky juice dribble down his chin. The meat of the fruit was sweet and firm. He used the bread to catch the juice. "I've never tasted anything like this," he said.

"It's grown by the sea, ripened by the sun. It will give you strength for the long journey ahead." Michaal offered him a drink.

Icharitas paused. "I know nothing about this world. Not even how I happen to be here. Tell me."

"Ask us what you want to know," said Hospadar, a burly man with a wide, kindly face.

"Tell me about these long flat strips we are on. They seem to stretch for miles."

"Once these roadbeds joined the Medieglot with your world," Hospadar explained.

"The Medieglot?"

"Centuries ago, the Medieglot was linked to Europe by these corridors, but they are no longer used."

"The Medieglot?" he repeated.

"Middle Earth. The land that lies between north and south. Surely you must know that term?"

The Medieglot. Of course. Icharitas's mind reeled. His thoughts spun over, and in a rush, the world of Centrex caught up with him.

Richard was leaning forward in his chair. There was Mel, dominating the conversation, as usual. "But that part of the world is barren..." Mel was arguing.

Icharitas felt a hand shaking his shoulder.

"Are you all right?"

He shook himself free of his memory. His head pounded. He was in the Medieglot!

He looked at the others, none of whom seemed to find anything amiss. "I'm fine," he said. He took a handful of walnuts. Centrex was fading. Before his recollection of it faded completely, he tried one more question. "So, how did I come to be here?"

"It's a mystery." Sequitus grinned as he started packing away the food. "More walnuts?"

"No, thank you." Icharitas looked at him, then looked back at Michaal.

"Come, Ichar," said Michaal. "We have a long journey ahead of us."

He nodded. It was hard here to keep his mind on anything but what was directly in front of him. He felt so bewildered. Who were these beings? How had they known to come and meet him? Why wouldn't they answer his questions? What did they want with him?

The men formed up on both sides of him and marched in step with him as they started down the road. Ichar lengthened his stride, they lengthened theirs. The walking was pleasant. To celebrate the rhythm, Richard began to hum quietly. The others joined in. No matter what their reason was for coming to meet him, these men were fine company. It was the first time he'd ever been surrounded by happy voices; the first time, he realized, he'd felt not alone.

Richard was overcome with pleasure. The wind blew on

his arms and face. Goldenrod shone beside the road; grass in the little glades was greener than a dream. His joy showed in the long, loping stride he set. Michaal took up the rhythm. The group was in tune.

Ugly laughter rang inside his head, Mel's laughter. *"The Medieglot is the center of betrayal, the place where Cain kills his brother Abel."* He felt himself stumble, his happy confidence shattering. Suddenly he wondered how far they had walked this day. His leg muscles were taut and a dull ache was beginning in his knees.

Then he was aware of Michaal. There was a look of concern in his eyes and he put his hand on Ichar's shoulder. "We'll stop here for the night."

"We've come a long way, haven't we?" asked Ichar.

"Here, lie on this." Hospadar was spreading a blanket under the trees. "Your legs will be stiff by morning if they're not looked after."

Ichar lay down and felt Hospadar's strong hands begin to knead his tired muscles. He liked this man's deep mellow voice and knowing touch. *Here I am in the Medieglot,* he mused, *and it's flowing with life.* He closed his eyes as Hospadar worked on his tired legs. As he drifted off into sleep, voices started in his head.

"One day someone will have the courage to enter the Medieglot," a woman's voice stated firmly.

"There he betrayed himself," mocked another voice.

"This time it will be different." The woman's voice was less certain.

"He will call forth an age long prophesied," said an older man's voice.

"But what if he himself is the one who betrays?" This voice was cold.

Ichar felt a chill pass through him. He turned over in his sleep and discovered his blanket had rolled off him. It was early morning, and he ached from a nightmare he couldn't recall. He lay there, his eyes closed, trying to get a sense of where he was. Voices now came from close around him.

"Are you are sure he can be trusted?"

"As I am his guardian. Did he not pass the test at Centrex? Did he not reach out at world's end? Yes, I stand by him."

"But that was a rehearsal. When the time comes..."

He stirred and the voices fell quiet. He opened his eyes and there beside him was Michaal, a worried look on his face.

The next evening, they sat for a long time by the fire, talking of the day's sightings – of a green lion and the many birds – and enjoying the wind from the south. Tonight was their last night. Tomorrow before nightfall, Michaal said, they would reach the coastline and their journey's end.

Ichar looked at David, who was staring dreamily into the fire. He was a lean, lanky man, wild and shy like a deer. "I have been thinking..." David's voice faltered; the firelight glistened in his eyes. Ichar moved closer, listening to the crackle of the flames. Finally the young man spoke again. "I would father a child."

Ichar felt as if his own most secret wish had been drawn from him. But before he could speak, he saw in the flames a woman's red hair, and suddenly he was back with her again. Pamela was looking directly into his face. He flinched as he remembered in full their last night together. He had come into her room. She had been lying there waiting for him.

There had been little need for words. Both of them had been drawn into a fierce embrace, a need for closeness. The moment of union had been sweet beyond belief, until he had raised himself and she had looked into his eyes. What had she seen there? Her sudden stillness had sent him fleeing to hide in his studio. But when he'd flung open the door and had seen what was there...

The embers flashed into a blaze as David added another log. Now Ichar could see only flames obliterating everything, everything he had ever held dear.

Ichar awakened late, the events of the night before vanishing quickly from his mind. Michaal and the others were almost packed. Slowly he got to his feet. His legs ached from this unaccustomed exercise. Michaal came over and handed him his pack. "Come, my friend, we are almost there. The wind has changed."

The wind now blew salty and moist. Though they marched for hours, it seemed to Ichar his feet barely touched the ground; he felt no tiredness, only the flowing pleasure of motion. Michaal led them along the river, then up over a height of land. Over the far descending ridge, Ichar saw a line of brilliant blue.

"The sea, Ichar," Michaal said as he broke into a run.

"Double pace!" shouted Raheem. The others took up the cry.

"Double pace!" shouted Ichar. They were off.

Ichar felt carried forward by some joyful massing of emotion. He sang out. The other men joined in his singing and their voices rolled down the valley, echoed over the hills. Onward they charged, singing, laughing, chanting. Down the steep slope they ran, hot and sweaty. They smashed into the sea, and the waves broke over them, cool, delicious, caressing. There they lay, motionless, staring skyward, their bodies lifting and falling with the surf.

Finally, they got out and dried themselves. They began to move southward along the gradually rising cliffs. Ichar looked out across the sea, marveling at its exquisite blue, so clear he was able to see schools of fish swimming beneath the surface. Ahead, he could see the land extending out into a long peninsula.

"It's not much farther," Michaal informed him. Suddenly they stopped at the cliff edge. There, directly below them, hidden from view until the moment before, was a steep-sided inlet. A tiny village nestled at the end of it.

"There it is, Ichar. Fino – the most beautiful spot in the world." Ichar gazed at the translucent blue of the inlet, at the boats floating as if on air, at the soft color of the ancient buildings.

"Look at it, Ichar!" Michaal was standing beside him.

Ichar noticed the tall cypresses across the bay, the thick stands of oak. An old castle, a circular ruin on the hillside across from the town, shone in the sunlight like a fortress of gold.

After a while, Michaal asked, "Are you ready?"

"Yes," replied Ichar. "I'm ready." He gazed down at the promenade in the center of town. It was filled with people, looking up, waving.

"Ichar." Michaal's arm was around his shoulder. "We've come a long way." Slowly and silently, like a warrior returning with a great prize, he led him off the hilltop, down the steep path.

People started to appear from every direction. Below him, Ichar could hear shouting, doors opening, the sound of running footsteps.

When they entered the square, he felt a youthful shyness. He saw Hospadar's big hand gently touch a face, saw David run through the crowd, heard delight in a woman's voice.

He looked around and noticed they were standing by a broken fountain. The statue or whatever it was that had carried the water upward was missing. There was no water carrier to stand upon the stone plinth. The water, what little there was of it, simply trickled out of a crack in the masonry base.

Suddenly a woman came up and hugged Michaal. Then she put her hand in Ichar's. She was all soft, fleshy folds, with crinkling eyes. "I'm Moira. Welcome."

A hush fell over the crowd. Ichar felt as if everyone were looking at him. Michaal said, "The lost has been found," and a deep peace, calming as the sea, came over him. He felt a great bond between himself and Michaal that both confused and humbled him. Ichar suddenly realised he was very tired.

"He's practically asleep on his feet, Moira." Michaal smiled at him proudly.

A young man of about eighteen approached and gazed at Michaal worshipfully, like a younger brother.

"Iden, I think it would be fitting if you acted as personal escort for Ichar."

"It would be an honor," Iden replied.

Iden's tanned body and blond hair reminded Ichar of Mel, of all that was best and untainted about his old friend. Ichar put his arm around Iden's shoulder. One day, he hoped, he would see Mel again.

He let himself be escorted away to a large, richly decorated room. Now that he was alone with Iden and Moira, he realized that the crowd had indeed overwhelmed him. He let gentle hands open his tunic. He lay in the bath and let them wash away the weariness of his journey, and afterward let them shave him, towel his body dry. He lay on the bed and felt them smooth a cool and refreshing ointment on his skin, enjoyed the touch of their hands as they massaged his back and legs. When the voices faded, he lay on the bed, relaxed.

They woke him as the sun was setting and dressed him. The robes caressed his body like a woman's hands. "It's linen," Iden told him. "There's to be a feast in your honor this evening."

Then Michaal arrived and escorted him to the square. Ichar felt shy under the gaze of so many eyes. He looked down and paid attention to the soft swish of his garments. He wondered what on earth he was doing here, why these people were taking such pains with him. He glanced across the square. The entire area was filled with people. They were all looking toward him. Candles flickered everywhere.

Michaal led him to the head table, which was set up near the sea, facing the square. Someone pressed a chair against the back of his legs. He tried not to look at the assembled faces. What on earth do they want of me? he wondered. He wondered why they were being so kind to him. It was hard to grasp what was happening to him.

He was interrupted from his reverie by Michaal.

"Wine, Ichar?"

Ichar nodded and held out his glass. Michaal poured a golden liquid into the tall, stemmed goblet.

"It's the nectar of the gods," came a voice from down the table. Ichar searched along the table and finally found Hospadar's broad face smiling at him. "To you!" Hospadar said, raising his glass.

Ichar took a sip. The drink had a cold edge that cut the thickness in his mouth. He drained the glass in two gulps. He felt refreshed, alert.

Ichar gazed across the square again. The number of people in the space seemed immense, a vast multitude, assembled to – to do what? He stared back at his glass.

"Aren't the glasses beautiful?" asked Moira, leaning toward him. "We found them here when we arrived. They're hundreds of years old."

"In the north we use disposables," said Ichar.

Moira smiled at him but didn't say anything. He suddenly wondered if she knew what a "disposable" was. Michaal poured him another glassful of wine.

Ichar studied the multitude. He searched for a streak of grayness, a touch of flabbiness. He could not see any. He studied the faces. Each one was different; each reflected a unique being. They would expect him to speak. What did they want him to say?

He heard Michaal push back his chair. The speeches were beginning. What could he say? He had nothing to give them.

"It is an honor to welcome the ambassador from the north among us." Michaal turned toward him and held him with his eyes. "Your arrival marks a moment of great significance for us. You bring us hope of a new beginning." Michaal raised his glass. "It is you, Icharitas, we celebrate this evening. To you, who have traveled beyond time and space, I say well met and welcome amongst us."

"To you," came the voices.

He could see them lifting glasses. He closed his eyes and tried to relax. Their warmth and goodwill flowed through him and heartened him.

He stood up. He still did not know what he was going to say. He raised his own goblet, lifted it high, and then, on impulse, moved it from east to west. The words rose unbidden: "For each of you, I stand here, a pledge. For each of you, fulfilment."

"New life and safe return," came the response.

He sat down. Food was now brought. Ichar watched a woman walk to their table and put down a huge tureen. She smiled at him. Ichar gazed at her as she walked away. She was tall, with long auburn hair; she was the most beautiful woman he had ever seen.

"That's Delana," Moira informed him. "She prepared this meal for you." His heart overflowed with gratitude.

Covered platters were brought to the table. One opened to reveal a steaming white fish. Ichar wondered what this strange food would taste like. Hot pungent odors rose from bowls and serving dishes around him, thick and heavy as incense.

Moira ladled large portions onto his plate. "You'll find this better than anything you've ever tasted."

Around him people talked and laughed, passed food, drank. David caught his eye. He mimicked someone who thought the food tasted strange. Ichar laughed. David had read his thoughts again.

Ichar realised that he was very hungry. He picked up a silver fork and sampled one of the foods on his plate. He chewed; a buttery flavor opened in his palate. He took a bite of bread and then a forkful of fish. Moira was right: he'd never tasted food like this before in his life. He wiped his lips, helped himself to more. He washed the meal down with another glass of wine. He could never tire of food like this. Delana had indeed prepared him a feast.

She came toward him bearing a tray of fruit. "Thank you," he said.

"Thank you!" she replied. Her face was close to his; it was radiant. He wondered if she knew her eyes were as green as emeralds. Suddenly her eyes twinkled as though she possessed a great and wonderful secret. Then she moved off, down the table.

Ichar turned to Michaal. "This is so magnificent – here, the Medieglot." He gestured with a piece of bread, at a loss for words.

Michaal nodded. "It may be hard for you to understand, and it is certainly difficult to explain." He gestured in turn. "We were forced out of linkage with the space and time dimensions of your world. We wait here for a return to that plane. We wait, hoping the vibrations will change enough to allow us to enter."

"How will that come about?"

"It all depends on people like you. How did you manage to come here?"

"For me it was through time. Though time is invisible, it, too, is a dimension. You can disappear into it by either slowing down or speeding up." Ichar realized how much he enjoyed talking about time transport.

Hospadar leaned forward. "Because our rhythm here is different, we live on a higher plane."

Ichar now understood their plight. Because of their vibratory level, they were unable to enter the dense plane of his world. "Before you could return and reunite with mankind, earth's vibratory level would have to increase to a new level," he said. He wished Hornepayne were here with him. These were the kind of discussions his mentor loved.

Heads nodded.

"For some, such a change would feel like death," Hospadar commented. "For others, though – for the ones

71

who were ready – such a change would open up so much."

"You will return to earth one day," Ichar said quietly.

"We hope so," said Michaal.

Ichar was interrupted by the sound of silver chiming against crystal. Hospadar tapped his spoon against his wine goblet. "To the woman who gave us this feast."

"To the man who gives us cause to feast," Delana's voice rang back.

Hospadar stood and waited for silence. "Food blessed by the sun and served by loving hands..." His voice was resonant. "One day may all peoples eat of such food, be nourished by earth and sun, and be one with one another. Heaven and earth, angels and men – living one with the other. Let it be so."

Everyone fell into a chant that to Ichar seemed to be a single word. Sometimes it sounded like 'home,' sometimes like 'all men,' at other times like 'woman.' He felt filled with a bliss that deepened to a silent peace.

Into the calm that settled across the square, Hospadar came forward and took his place beside the broken fountain. An ancient text was brought forward. Hospadar read of a time yet to come, of an earth radiant with awakened life, of an end to the ancient enmity between light and darkness.

Ichar felt an exaltation that he needed to share. He remembered the word he'd heard that night he'd recalled the voice of his father. Ichar sang the word in his heart, then he sang it aloud. "Alleluia!"

The group received it and shared it with him. Out over the world the song flowed, until a quiet hush settled over them.

Ichar sat back, heard again the lap and sigh of the sea behind him, felt a sweet peace overcome him. He looked out across the sky and noticed that the moon had risen, full, a perfect circle. Beside him, Michael was talking. He listened sleepily.

"Once so long ago that it is beyond memory, came the splitting of life into day and night. Long has the struggle between light and darkness raged. Times there have been of sunlight, times of winter and darkness. But now begins a new season: the union of both. Here with us is man – man who has accumulated the fullness of both – standing astride day and night. For us he is the bridge. Man is the one by whom the impossible will be made possible. Long have we awaited his maturing. Now the future is held in his hands.

"We can help. We can give him our strength. Yet all depends on him, on the free choosing of his race. By his deed will we enter his plane that the promise may be fulfilled, that spirit and flesh may be as one."

Ichar suddenly understood. By the work of his hands it would come to pass. He would do that part, he resolved. He caught sight of Delana, standing beside one of the far tables. It would be for her that he would do whatever they asked.

Overhead the moon hung, a lucent pearl within the star-filled night.

Chapter Four

Pamela sat chilled and cold on the hard wooden bench as the ancient Hovercraft thumped across the bay toward Dublin, the sole entrance to Enclave Ireland. The whining of the air jets and the smell of the diesel fuel made her feel ill, but she forced down the nausea. To distract herself, she turned and examined the scene out the window. At first she could see nothing but fog and dull, tossing sea, but after a few minutes, coastal hills came into sight, low and blackened by rain clouds.

She remembered how once, long ago, she had wanted to escape those soft hills, to be free, to discover the world of her father. Centrex had not been what she had expected. She was glad to be returning. She belonged here in this benighted land so mired in the past.

The young student beside her reached under the bench for his briefing kit. He was coming from Centrex on an observation program. She had met hundreds of these eduprobes wandering around Ireland, poking, asking questions, examining everything as if it were an object in a museum.

Centrex had seen fit to grant Ireland the "freedom" to

close its boundaries. In truth, Centrex had quarantined her island, encouraged its citizens to hold fast to their old beliefs and religions; made it, in fact, a sealed showcase of a past culture, displayed like an ant colony between two glass plates.

The intercom voice broke into her thoughts. "You will disembark at one o'clock enclave time." Then it repeated the message it had broadcast every half hour throughout the trip. Pamela tried not to listen, but it was hard not to pay attention to the recorded voice. "You are entering a carefully controlled environment of people and culture, one century past. The inhabitants have been voided of all curiosity and programmed nonaggressive. Enclave Ireland is a primitive sociodrama of the early twentieth century. This opportunity has been provided by the Centrex Cultural Coordination Committee. We repeat. You are entering a carefully controlled environment..." The voice went on and on.

Pamela's back hurt. She could not bear the thought of being used. She resented the presence of the student eduprobe beside her. Perhaps even more, she resented her people, who were always so willing and pleasant. The eduprobe tried to catch her eye, to share a smile with her, but she turned away and stared stonily back out the portal. A shaft of sunlight hit the somber hills, transformed them to a soft green. When the sun shone, there was such a mysterious beauty to this place of bogs and rain.

Her mother would be by the hearth waiting for her. They would drink tea and talk. Pamela reflected on that comfortable childhood world. She would never go back to Centrex.

She had been stupid to have gone in the first place. The reasons she had made the journey – to find her father, to discover the reasons he had left, to convince him to return home again – seemed foolish to her now.

The Hovercraft moved onto the platform and hit the mooring pad with a thud. Now Richard, too, had left her. He was just like her father. She hated them both. The pressure lock opened and moist, earthy air entered. Neither of them had given her a thing. She pushed her way forward out into the air and through the entry procedures. Well, never again. She was home and she was planning to stay.

Pamela strode up Connolly Street. The putrid odors of the river seemed to her starved senses like the essence of life itself. Here was mud and river and sea. Here was home.

She turned down a lane and gazed into store windows, recognizing knits, plaids, real leather shoes. She smiled to herself with pleasure.

Wasn't that a familiar face? Wasn't that Mrs. Coughlin? It was all coming back to her now. She ran across the cobbles, shouting; the woman stopped, turned. The eyes seemed to look right through her.

"I must have been mistaken," Pamela muttered.

She turned back onto Connolly Street and noticed an old woman coming toward her. Pamela smiled and greeted her in Gaelic. The reply came back to her toneless, without a smile.

Everything seemed very confusing. Had something happened since she'd been away? The sun disappeared behind a cloud bank and the street grew suddenly drab and dreary. Perhaps she needed to sit and collect her thoughts. She stepped off the curb to cross over to the park, but the clanking of the tram startled her. She had to run to get beyond the track, out of the way. She noticed on the rear platform the eduprobe who had sat beside her on the Hovercraft. He smiled and waved at her. She ignored him.

She began to run, it didn't matter where. After a few minutes, she arrived at the steps of the old cathedral.

"*Mea culpa, mea culpa, mea maxima culpa.*" Beyond the altar rail, the ancient Roman rituals of the church were being celebrated. She watched as the shrunken little priest, gnarled by age, begged forgiveness for their sins. It was comforting to be hidden in the cathedral's darkness. She could smell a hint of incense. She watched as the priest raised the vessel containing the blood of Christ and offered it that the world would one day be redeemed.

She heard the words that transformed wine to blood, the bread to life. But nothing happened. The words echoed emptily, without magic. She looked about her in horror. The priest was powerless; he didn't believe.

The church was half-full but no one seemed to have noticed. They came, they prayed, but the spirit had gone from them. She felt a wave of panic. For a moment she stood, stunned by the scene. Then she genuflected, blessed herself and ran down the worn stone steps, her eyes dimmed with tears.

A dream she had had as a child entered her mind – or was it a story her mother had once told her? Some fishermen had found a boat adrift far out in the Atlantic. Everyone was at his station, manning the sails, steering, in the galley – but everyone was dead except for a little girl, whom they found talking to the dead as if they were alive. They took her back to the village, but she remained demented until the day she threw herself into the sea.

Pamela made her way to the railway station and bought a one-way ticket to Galway. It would be different at home. Her mother would understand. She hated this museum of stone-cold mummies. She felt hatred of anything to do with Centrex. She could not even begin to think about Richard. Most of all, she hated herself, Pamela Duggan, bought, sold, used, discarded. "Leave me alone!" she shouted when a passerby, arms filled with brown shopping bags, bumped into her.

The trip to Galway was a relief after her experiences in Dublin. The clicking of the train's wheels lulled her into drowsiness. She fell at last into deep, desperately needed sleep. She awoke to find herself in the station of slow-moving Galway. She sat in her seat, blinking awake. Her eyes idled on a man pulling a freight wagon slowly across the platform. His back was bent, his gaze downward like an automaton. She could not take her eyes off him. There was a stillness in the air; she sensed decay.

She collected her luggage, but just as she realized she had told no one of her arrival, out of the corner of her eye she caught sight of a familiar pair of baggy corduroys coming toward her.

"Jamie O'Ryan!"

"Pammie Duggan!" He smiled down at her and then caught her in a huge hug.

She leaned against his chest, felt tears in her eyes.

"What's this?" he said, stepping backward, looking down at her.

"Oh, Jamie. I feel as though I'm going crazy."

He took her belongings and brought them around to the back of his wagon. When he returned, he reached out and touched her shoulder.

"Hop up now. We'll have plenty of time on the road to talk." He escorted her around to the righthand side of his horse and wagon, helped her climb on.

Suddenly she remembered. "Jamie!"

He turned to face her.

"How did you know I was coming?"

He smiled. "I just had a feeling."

A strange strength came from this man. She no longer felt afraid. She looked down into his soft gray eyes. He had always been there for her, ever since she could remember. Whenever she was hurt, the time she had got lost... He knew her in a way she didn't understand.

"I don't know why I deserve such a guardian angel!"

Jamie just laughed and flapped the reins. She looked away from him. She felt so confused and upset.

The small horse slowly drew the cart into the country-side. She recognized the familiar lines of moss-buried rock, the old crumbling fences that kept the sheep in their places. At a bend in the road, Jamie reined in the horse.

Beside them stood a large rectangular stone with a crudely

shaped hole in its center. The early farmers had been unable to move it, so had simply incorporated it into the line of the fence. Pamela gazed dreamily through the hole to the patch of green pasture beyond.

The stone spoke of eons. Generation upon generation had come and gone before its making had been completed; ages of softening by sun and rain and wind. Now it stood, of the fence but not fence, both wall and portal. Through it, sunlight suddenly splashed the pasture bright green.

"It's just big enough for a child to crawl through!" she exclaimed.

Suddenly the wind took her hair and she laughed in delight. The wind carried with it the salty tang of the sea. She stood to see if she could catch a glimpse of the coast, but the hills around them were too high.

"It will not be easy, but I will be with you."

Pamela looked down into Jamie's warm eyes, sat back down, then put her hand into his open palm. The panic left her.

"I'm ready now. Let's go on."

He picked up the reins. "Your mother won't be expecting you, you know," he said quietly. Pamela felt a strange feeling stir in her. "She has always been flint to your stone."

"True," Pamela said. There had never been much warmth between them.

"Still, she's done you a great service."

Pamela nodded, unsure of what he meant. So close to home, she wasn't sure she wanted the trip to end.

Her mother poured her another cup of tea and sat back. "Now tell me again. You did enjoy yourself in the north?"

"I've told you all about it. What more is there to say?" Pamela watched as her mother ate yet another crust loaded with jam.

"Tell me," the older women said, licking jam off her fingers, "Is it really true they keep idiot girls to use as breeders? That they keep them locked away deep underneath the ice?"

"Don't go on with your silly questions! Yes, it's true that most of the men can't give a woman a child. It's true they use sperm banks from the past." She remembered Richard, that last night they'd spent together. Her mother would never learn anything from her about Richard.

"It's a great pity that men should lose their manhood." Her mother smiled shyly. "I'd love to go there myself and tell those men a thing or two."

"You know well enough you're just an enclave!" Pamela snapped. "You know you'd never be allowed to leave Ireland."

"That's not my meaning – you know that." The older woman glared at her. "You still see me only as your foolish old mother. That's the truth, isn't it?"

"Jamie tells me your house is full of eduprobes. Really – renting your rooms to those people. It's disgusting! Surely, if you want dirt, you can get it from them."

"If they tell me things, I tell them a few things back," she snapped. "If they came here for learning, they leave with a little more than they expected. They give me a living –

thanks be to God for that. But still, I get lonely with you being away in the north."

"Mother, stop! You know I had to go. You made me!"

But the older woman wasn't listening. "When you were away I got to thinking of your father. I don't suppose you saw him, did you?"

"Why would you think that?" Pamela demanded. She could feel a crazy anger creeping through her. There seemed no way to get through to her mother. Suddenly she exploded. "For heaven's sakes! How could I go and see him? How could I find him? You never even gave me his name! The truth is that I never had a father – and you never had a husband!" Pamela was crying now. "It's time you grew up and faced the facts!"

Her mother straightened with a calm dignity. "Pamela," she said. "Listen to me. Your father entered my life for but a short time. But he gave me love – real honest love. He came and he gave me you. And that has made all the difference. It is you who needs to grow up. You who needs to face the facts."

"I don't want to hear any more about men! Do you hear me?" Pamela stood before her mother, shaking.

"Daughter of mine, filled with a dark rage ever since the day you were born. I will not tell you more. But will you not let someone in?"

Pamela pushed down her self-pity. What her mother didn't know was that she had let someone in, and that now she was lost. She would not give in to anyone ever again. A plague on them all!

Her mother gazed at her. Finally the older woman said wearily, "Perhaps you'd be more comfortable at Miss McCracken's?"

"It's so fine being home," Pamela muttered.

Her mother looked at her, then sighed and turned toward the peat fire.

Pamela finally broke the silence. "Have my things sent over as soon as you can."

It was days before Pamela felt herself over the anger that had erupted that day with her mother. She set herself to making a home of the room at Miss McCracken's. It proved quite adequate, except for one thing: after the second day, she started to become aware of a slight odor.

"I don't smell a thing," was her landlady's reply.

Pamela felt bewildered. She went to the market, but the odor swirled about her even in the streets and lanes. A friend of her mother's came up to her. The reek was overpowering. Pamela turned and ran. Why would they not wash themselves? she wondered – but she knew the smell did not arise from lack of washing.

She stopped some children who were skipping. "Let me skip with you."

They looked at her queerly, but because she was an adult, they agreed.

"One hundred and one. One hundred and two. One hundred and three."

She would skip on and on. She looked at their faces. They thought she was crazy. But she wasn't. Her foot caught in the rope.

"It's your turn to spin," said one of them.

She began to turn the rope and count. As long as she was counting, she was free of what was bothering her.

Then it was suppertime. She wandered on and the odor returned. She ran back to her room, but the reek was still on her skin. She scrubbed herself clean in a hot bath and went to bed. She awoke later in the dark, suffocating in the odor of decay and death. She thought of the little girl who had thrown herself into the sea. She got out of bed, dressed.

She ran toward the sea. She would fling herself in, purify herself in its salty depths, be done with herself – freed, finally, of everything. There was the sea in front of her, just beyond the rocks. A woman's voice stopped her. "Hail, full of grace. Blessed art thou, woman."

Pamela looked about her. The moon was rising. Its pale, pearly light transformed the scene and revealed a hunched figure, silvered by moonlight, perched high above her on a huge rock, facing outward toward the sea.

The old woman chanted on. "Hail Mary, who are in heaven. Hail full of grace. Hail fruit of thy womb. Pray for us now in this, the time of our deliverance."

The old woman's voice fell silent, and Pamela felt peace entering her. She settled herself quietly in the shadow and listened as the old woman began again.

So passed the Midsummer vigil, the night of longest day. When the moon dropped behind the sea cliffs, the old woman got up and headed down the road toward Kinvarra.

Hesitantly, Pamela climbed up and took her place, listening to the sea heave and thrash against the rock. The steady waves of sound beat against her; she felt the sea jump upward, felt its pulse shiver through her. The waters' breathing surged upward, began to wash away the contagion, to lull her into a gentle sleep.

Pamela woke to the crisp perfume of the morning sea in her nostrils. She had dreamed a strange dream. She'd returned to the church of her baptism with a lighted candle. By its light, she'd become aware above her of a statue of a madonna. The statue's right hand was raised, a beacon for the sailor lost at sea.

Pamela stood up on the rock, stretched awake. She no longer felt buried alive. She walked back from the sea, suspended between dream and waking. Quietly she climbed the back stairs to her room.

"Would you like to come down for a bite of breakfast?" Miss McCracken's words rose through the floor.

"Thank you. I'll be down in a minute," she shouted back. The old nausea assailed her; squeamishness caught her unexpectedly. She hurried to the toilet. Then she took herself downstairs for breakfast. Miss McCracken's eyes searched her. "A cup of hot tea will make you feel a little better, dear. You were late coming in. You're not feeling sickly, are you, child?"

"No, I'm in good health." She nibbled at a piece of toast. When Miss McCracken continued to stare, Pamela answered more firmly. "I'm quite well, thank you."

"I looked through your room in case there was a dead

mouse, but I found nothing but the scent of clean linen."

Pamela looked at Miss McCracken as from a great distance.

"Don't be getting angry with me!" the woman hurried on. "I was only concerned for your own good – seeing as you had mentioned it to me." She eyed her cautiously. "You came in late last night...."

"I went for a walk because I didn't feel like sleeping. That's all."

"That's not a proper thing for a girl in your condition to be doing...." Miss McCracken's voice hung, questioning.

Pamela studied the woman who sat across the table from her. She put her cup down carefully. "If you'll excuse me – " she got to her feet " – I've things to do."

"Certainly, my dear." Miss McCracken offered her a smile. "You go right ahead."

Pamela stood on the stoop, glad to be outside. She felt the warmth of the sun, even though it was hidden behind the eaves. She decided to visit the market square.

Some tinkers had brought down horses to sell. She gazed at the large beasts, snorting and shaking their manes, keeping away the flies. She studied the gypsy wagons, decorated with the zodiac; watched the gypsies sitting beside their fires, their clothes bright, their eyes clear. They, too, had their secrets.

Pigeons wheeled and somersaulted, white against the blue sky. She longed to be aloft, afloat on the winds. She was born to fly; home was out there in the heavens. Yet here she was, a prisoner in this benighted land. A group of children came past, taunting her. She looked at them, saddened; adults had got to them. At the market, she drifted about the stalls, handling the summer fruit.

"Well, if that woman thinks she can pull the wool over my eyes...!" Pamela heard Miss McCracken's voice in the next stall. "The nerve of her, planning to have her baby right here in my house. She isn't much different from her mother, I'll tell you that much. There was a time when her Alice was packing to go down to County Cork for the same reason."

They were talking about her. She put down a shilling for an apple and strode out of the market. She stopped to look at the horses again. What magnificent creatures! She thought of the gossip. People would talk; would accuse her of sinning not only against God, but against her own people. They would band together until they were swarming like angry hornets or shrill fishwives. Finally, they would cast her out. She presented her apple to a handsome nut-brown cob. He ate it with relish. She stroked his mane, enjoying the warm softness. Then she wandered, aimless, through the back lanes.

Miss McCracken had gone to visit Monsignor Kirby; it had been agreed that the old priest would visit Pamela. His visit made the rumor official. That morning, when Pamela came back to her room, Miss McCracken broke off all niceties and told her she would be expected to find another place by the weekend. The first stone had been cast.

Pamela went for supper to Fermanagh's Diner, only to

have their little girl ushered into the back and the meal served in silence. When she was finished, she walked up the lane where she had played as a child.

She found herself in front of her mother's house. How she longed at that moment to enter that house, to be held and comforted by her mother, to let her heart go. She knocked and entered. The living room smelled musty. She examined the faded wallpaper and listened to her mother chatter. Then she sat in the old rocking chair and moved back and forth. Distant, she waited for the next stone to be cast.

"You're with child, Pamela."

She stopped rocking, nodded.

"Do you want it?"

"I don't know."

"Well, if you want it to be born, you'll have to rid yourself of your rage. You know what I mean."

Pamela nodded.

"You're no longer a little girl. Make your choices as you will. But remember the life within you is sacred, and remember, too, that I love you."

Pamela walked over to her mother and held her close. She sensed a strength passing to her. Then, taking her shawl, she walked past her mother, out into the evening. That embrace was the most she could allow herself.

She walked on, out of the village. There was always the sea, she reminded herself. She didn't want to bring a child into this world. She thought back to that evening with Richard as she walked in the dark along the seawall.

She wanted to laugh. Fate had played her a cruel joke. She had gone north to confront her father; instead, it was Richard she met. Now she was pregnant with his child. Pamela felt caught in a sticky web. She seethed with stubborn anger.

When the morning fishermen met her on the road, they made way and blessed themselves. Her eyes were cast ahead, fierce with intent. She passed like a woman possessed. Day after day, she wandered up the coast, sleeping by the roadside, begging in hamlets or going hungry. She had to find the old woman she had met on the rock. She would have answers. But the crone seemed to have vanished from the earth. Pamela searched for weeks, and as she searched, a plan began to form slowly in her mind.

Then one day she found a place she knew was right. The little structure stood high on the brow of a hill like a beacon, overlooking the sea. It was the sunlight glancing off the tin roof that first attracted her; in that brief moment, the place shone like a castle of gold.

She climbed up to the front of the earthen-gray building. It was a deserted chapel, smaller than a stone cottage. It sat facing the Atlantic; a porch protected the arched doorway. Over the door, someone had chipped a prayer into the cracked masonry: *Stella Mare, ora pro nobis.* The chapel was built on a huge table rock. Here, she decided, she would have the child.

But first, she told herself, she would have to face the darkness that had been haunting her. She cleaned out the clutter of foul-smelling animal dirt and dead leaves from the interior and built a bed of dry moss. In the clean, sweet-smelling chapel she waited. Day after day through the late-summer afternoons, she sat on the porch, waiting. For nearly two weeks she ate nothing. Gradually, her hunger transformed from a bodily craving to a fierce inner sense of deprivation. Still she waited. A fierce stubbornness held her fast.

Sometimes as she waited she thought of her mother. Sometimes she thought of Richard. And sometimes, oddly enough, she thought of Hornepayne. Up in her hut, she felt cut off from everyone she had ever tried to care about. Even the sea and sky seemed too far away to give any comfort. And where was that old woman she had been counting on to save her?

Then, one dark night, the air heavy, the clouds swirling and massing, it happened. Her body, weakened by her fast, finally collapsed and gave up its inner secret. Her rage – starved, hungry, desperate – rose out of her body and faced her.

There, before her, was a woman, old, lined, fleshy. The woman's face was sullen; her dark shadowless eyes stared, hostile, straight into Pamela's. Pamela felt a rush of anger and aversion: this woman was all she hated most in her mother. But then she cried out in pain, for this woman was not only her mother, but also herself: spiteful, hostile, subservient.

With her shame came tears. And in her tears, the image dissolved, and Pamela stepped into that secret room in her heart, into that place she had always protected – virginal, inviolate, untouched and untouchable. That self that had always been free.

Whether asleep or awake, she knew not, but she began to hear voices, a choir of praise to a world yet unborn. She opened her eyes, and before her, she saw an orb, shining in the cosmos, a luminous pearl. Cleansed and quiet, filled with a tide of joyful anticipation, Pamela rose and waited for the dawn. Slowly, almost imperceptably, the eastern sky brightened.

The sun rose over the horizon, millions of times greater than herself, unimaginable in power and strength. She stood before it, frail but free. At last she was her own person, free to choose. She stepped forward to meet the dawn.

Chapter Five

Icharitas woke to find the sun streaming in his window. He kicked off the covers, yawned and noticed the sunlight shining on the ancient castle across from his window. He felt like a boy again. He rolled across the bed onto his feet, admired the large plant in the corner. "Well, my handsome, you look tall and happy this morning."

He went outside and looked across the square. It was empty of any sign of the feasting of the night before. *They must have cleared it away before I awoke*, he thought – or perhaps it had all been a dream.

"Hi!"

He turned around. It was Iden.

"Michaal said you might sleep late this morning."

"The best sleep I can remember. I feel fifteen years younger."

"You look like a great worry has been lifted from you." Iden pointed to a table at the high end of the square. "Breakfast is waiting."

Ichar found it hard to remember the night before, the beauty of the morning so overwhelmed him. He breathed in the fresh sea air. He noticed the ancient buildings that lined the street. Their faded green and pink fronts looked solid and comfortable.

"I can hardly believe this is happening to me. It's amazing! I no longer feel cold or gray."

Iden looked at him curiously.

"Iden, what causes the cobbles to sparkle like that?"

"It's the quartz in the cobblestones. It catches the sunlight, reflects it back to us. Beautiful, isn't it? Like a sea of diamonds."

"I can't believe it."

"The sun does marvelous things, even to stones."

They walked across the square, sat down at the breakfast table. Ichar tried to explain his feelings again. "Just sitting here, looking at the sun, smelling the sea...I have this sense that I'm going to blink and it will all just disappear."

"Don't blink then," Iden laughed.

"One has to blink." Ichar was annoyed. "You can't keep your eyes open forever."

"Maybe that's a way of fooling yourself."

"What is?"

"Closing your eyes to what is. Look how beautiful everything is." Iden laughed again. It all seemed so obvious to him. He reached over and poured cream on Ichar's peaches. Then he took the top off a clay container and spooned out a thick golden syrup. "Here, try some of this."

"What is it?" Ichar took the spoon, sniffed the heavy waxy odor suspiciously.

"It's honey."

"Honey?"

"Made by bees. It's as sweet on the tongue as love in the heart."

Ichar laughed, tasted it, puckered his lips. "Too sweet for my liking."

"Too sweet?" Iden looked stunned. "I could live on it."

Ichar put down the spoon, leaned forward on his elbows. "Iden, there's so much life in this world. Where does it come from?"

"Easy! Bees are great at it!" Iden picked up the spoon, licked it clean, reached for more. "Mmm. Liquid sunshine!" He buzzed over the pot, plunged the spoon into the honey, played with it, pulled it out dripping with golden fluid.

Ichar watched, fascinated. Who was this playful youth, so tanned and tousled? He returned to his point. "That doesn't make sense," he said indignantly. "There has to be a source."

"Of course there is, but it is everywhere. Michaal knows more of it; he is the guardian. I only know that the Medieglot is charged. All you need to do is to transform it, the way bees make honey from flowers, and trees make sap from sun and earth. It's really very simple."

Ichar nodded. If Iden wasn't going to tell him, he'd find out the truth for himself. Iden talked on, trying to explain how simple life was. Ichar finished his breakfast in silence.

The broken fountain again caught his eye. There was something missing. The bare plinth in the center bothered him. What had happened to it? Why had they left it looking so raw and damaged and why was there so little water flowing up from the center?

"Ichar, such thoughts are not becoming on a beautiful morning."

"What?" Ichar jumped as if he felt Iden's presence in his mind.

"Don't be so gruff and glum. It's such a beautiful day!"

Ichar forced himself to smile, tried to pull himself out of his thoughts.

Iden pointed skyward. "Look at the sky. Smell the air!"

He nodded reluctantly.

"So much to see. So much to do." Iden got up. "Michaal is out in the fields this morning. In the meantime, I am your friend and guide. Would you like to see what we do?"

Ichar got up slowly. "Show me the bees."

Iden laughed. "Come, I'll show you everything. You can see for yourself how it all works." He led him around the corner and into a low building.

A warm, heavy smell hit Ichar as he walked toward the building. "Enter into the first of our mysteries," said Iden, opening the door for him. The youth greeted the women who were working inside. "Ladies, we come that man may understand." He bowed elaborately and laughed.

Ichar looked about the room. The women's faces were white with flour. Before each of them, on the table, lay a white, shapeless mass.

"Come and join us then," one of the women called. "But be warned! There is more here than meets the eye."

Iden laughed. "Isn't that why we're here?"

"Come." Ichar saw one of the women gesturing to him. "Sit here. I'll show you."

Iden ushered Ichar to the table and presented him with a high stool. Ichar looked about.

"Hello, my darlings." Iden moved about. "We've come so you can show us the magic you possess." He grinned across at Ichar. "They're so beautiful I can't sit still."

Ichar admired his unabashed playfulness.

"I'm Leona," the girl beside him said. Then the woman next to her introduced herself.

"Stop," Ichar begged. "I won't remember a single name."

They ignored his plea. Names came tumbling at him. It was hopeless to try to remember them all. He started to laugh. After a moment they were all laughing.

When the laughter subsided, Ichar caught his breath. "So what is it that you do?" he asked.

"We work the dough," Leona explained. "In the dough is a yeast of millions of living cells. We push and pound this glob in front of us until it comes alive – like this. Watch."

She folded the mass of dough, then leaned over and pushed down with stiff arms on the fold she had made. Then she raised the dough head-high and smashed it onto the table top. She giggled at his concerned expression. "You can't be gentle with it. At least, not at this stage." She pushed the dough toward him. "Here. You try it."

He reached out and felt the humid warmth of the white mass, smelled the rich pungent odor of the yeast. He sank his fingers deep into the ferment. Somehow its touch reminded him of flesh: the touch of cool, soft female skin. He squeezed it, folded it toward him, enjoyed its heavy droopy weight, lifted it up, plopped it on the counter. His hands tingled. Push, turn, fold, pummel: soon he became absorbed in the rhythm about him. He began to sense life moving through what had been awhile ago inert matter. He felt excited to be helping to bring the dough to life.

A woman spoke to him from across the table. "You touched me very deeply last night."

Ichar nodded, kept his eyes on the dough, kneading and pounding.

"Yes," said another. "It was such an opening for joy."

Ichar patted the dough, felt it warm and springy and alive. He let himself smile.

"You know that your arrival has given us hope."

Ichar looked into the serious eyes beside him.

"We have been waiting for a way to enter your world."

Ichar imagined his world as a mass of inert dough, these souls laboring at it with loving hands. He sifted some flour over his dough. He looked around. He realized that he must be as white as the faces about him.

Iden brought in a rack of pans. The dough was ready for the next step. "Dough needs time to ripen," Leona explained. "So we will leave it here for a while. Then we will put it in these pans...and then into the oven. What comes out is bread fit for the gods."

Ichar thanked his new friends and withdrew with Iden to the square.

"Well?" Iden asked.

"I feel well kneaded."

Iden rolled his eyes at the pun.

Ichar stopped to rinse his hands in the fountain. He nodded toward the stump in the center of it. "By the way, what happened there?"

"When the fountain was destroyed, the water pretty much stopped flowing."

At that moment a flash of white appeared at the entrance to the inlet. Ichar recognized it as an ancient sailing boat. He held his breath as a gust of wind keeled the boat at a sharp angle. He watched as she crossed the inlet like an apparition in white, swept in close to the promenade, swung into the wind and dropped her sails. He was enthralled by her beauty and grace.

He shivered. He felt a blinding emotion rising within him. He pulled back, but remained shaken, troubled. Where had he seen this vessel before?

Iden held his arm comfortingly. "Are you okay?"

Ichar gained control of himself. He was back, safe in the sunlight.

"Yes, I'm fine." He tried to smile, but underneath he felt he was about to weep. "I don't know what came over me." He caught his breath. "I'm okay now. Thanks."

"Are you sure?"

"Yes, I'm sure."

Ichar was suddenly aware of people rushing by him. Women were wiping their hands on their aprons, men were clattering over the cobbles in wooden sandals.

Iden nudged him and smiled. "Come on then. Let's go and

watch." They joined the crowd running down to the wharf.

"Take a line; be quick about it," called a boisterous voice coming from the sailing ship. "It was a good morning. One of the best I can remember."

Ichar listened while Tommy told of the sea, of putting down lines into another world. The people on the wharf listened, commented, applauded as the fish were unloaded. Ichar enjoyed the fun around this morning ritual.

Finally he approached the man timidly. "Tommy," he said. "I'd like to go fishing with you."

"Any time! I'll be out again tomorrow; I'll be leaving before the moon goes down. If you want, I'll wake you."

"I'll be ready."

"You'll never be able to get up that early," Iden put in.

Ichar made a sign toward him with his fingers. They both laughed.

"What happened to old gruff and glum?"

Ichar grinned at Iden playfully. "I've no idea what you're talking about." They walked along the water's edge. Ichar looked down. The sea bottom seemed an arm's length away, yet he had the sense it was fathoms below the surface. Everything seemed so close, yet so far.

"It's nearly time to eat," Iden reminded him. "Michaal should be at the Phoenix by now. Remember? He wanted you to eat with him today."

"Great," said Ichar. He had so much to tell him. "How do I get there?"

"See that rock face overlooking the bay? See that opening at its base? That's the stairwell up to the Phoenix. It's a set of stone steps cut upward through a cleft in the rock. Climb those steps. They'll take you to Michaal." Iden waved at him and loped off toward the square.

Ichar walked over to the foot of the cliff. It took a moment for his eyes to adjust to the sudden shade. He put his hand on the cold iron rail and looked up at the steps, deeply hollowed by centuries of use. How many people before him had climbed them? He wondered if stone ever wore through. He put one foot forward and started up. The narrow stairwell was chill and smelled musty. He climbed slowly up the ancient cleft. Far above, he could see a small patch of light.

Finally, he came level with a garden patio. He eased up out of the passage and took off his sandals. The deep-hued rug laid out there felt rich and soft under his bare feet. He put his hand out to a huge wall-hanging, thick as a lion's mane. Before him, he could see stairs leading to a higher chamber. He paused, wandered over to the railing and looked out beyond the end of the inlet. Through the narrow mouth, he could see the deeper blue of the sea. Around the patio, he noticed several sculptures from antiquity. Masses of red and yellow flowers grew in planters along the railing.

"Welcome to the Phoenix, Ichar." Michaal was descending from upper rooms Ichar had noticed earlier. "Did you have a good morning?"

"I did. Iden showed me about. Tomorrow I hope to go out fishing."

Michael stood in front of him. For a split second, Ichar thought he was facing himself in the mirror. Then Michaal walked to the railing and leaned on it, looking out. Ichar followed; the sunlight felt warm on his shoulders.

"Your house is so beautiful. I never dreamed it would be like this."

"It's practically as we found it, you know. It was built over a hill spring by those who lived long before the Maelstrom."

"This morning...everyplace I go..." Ichar struggled for words. "Even the air is..."

Michaal laughed. "Some things won't be caught by words. You're right – there is something special about Fino."

"Am I imagining this world?" asked Ichar.

"It does at first seem unreal, like an enchanted land," Michaal explained.

"There has to be – to be more..." Ichar stumbled to a halt.

"Oh there is, much more." Michaal moved toward the chairs. Ichar sank into a soft blue one and felt it tilt back ever so slightly.

"I think you might better say that you enter this world through the imagination." Michaal's voice was warm, gracious. "I don't think you realize it, but we, too, are here as strangers. Fino's nature is a midpoint, a point of transport between two worlds. We are here awaiting entry into your world."

Food was brought in and they ate together. When they had finished, Ichar asked one of the questions that had been troubling him. "Michaal, the minds of Centrex deny this place exists."

"Here, in Fino, two worlds meet," he responded. "You

stand now on the outer limits of matter. Beyond this is spirit. We stand as close to matter as we are able. Until changes take place within your world, we are unable to enter."

Ichar must have looked confused.

"Let's try this another way." Michaal threw out his arms. "Stop thinking for a moment. Look. What do your eyes tell you?"

"I see a world undreamed of by Centrex…lush, verdant, happy. This is the kind of world I would dream of living in."

"Good," said Michaal. "You can see then that we operate here within a different, purer kind of energy. It can turn a man's mind unless he knows how to approach it, or unless he has a guide. You can see why it might be hard for Centrex to grasp what we are all about. But there is another reason Centrex denies us."

Ichar looked up, curious at the change in Michaal's voice.

"That reason is because our coming will ring the death knell for Centrex."

"But why?" said Ichar.

"It has to do with power," Michaal said. "You see, we offer a power that is beyond control." Ichar's friend thought for a moment. "Remember the tale of the boy who disobeyed his father and flew too near the sun? Well, what happened?"

"He fell to his death."

"He had not learned how to channel his new power; to learn that power is not a matter of use, but of service. Centrex does not serve, it controls. This is the heart of the matter."

Michaal got up, cleaned the leaves of a plant with his hands. "This fuchsia, for instance – it simply lets the sun flow into it. At the same time, it draws the elements of the earth inward to join with the sun. It controls neither. It simply transforms both into a new creation." He held the flower in his hand.

"But we're not plants," Ichar said, exasperated.

Michaal came back and sat across from him again. "Yet plants do have something to tell us."

Ichar felt uncomfortable.

"I dream of a time when we can all start over – a second chance," Michaal continued. "I would one day stand before the Prince of Darkness, Lucifer himself. I see us not warring, but embracing." Michaal came out of his reverie. "Ichar, I want your world to know the joy of the real world."

"But the other world *is* the real world."

"You have come from that world: you know how much suffering there is. Here is a reality mankind can choose."

"But Centrex is real; it is a fact. Without its control, the planet would destroy itself."

"That is how it seems to Centrex. But what if the world of Fino suddenly appeared? What would the computons do if they suddenly discovered a place of trees and birds and sun? Tell me, Icharitas. What would they do if they discovered a place they could not control, a place where power was in the air for everyone to use as freely as breathing, a place where joy is the rule, happiness the reality? Tell me, what would they do?"

Ichar got up and walked across the patio. The other world. It would...amuse itself with Fino, probe it, explain it, abuse it and, in the end, kill it. He felt sick inside. "They would destroy it!" he admitted.

"You see, Centrex has no love for life. Can you not see the contradictions? Centrex could not allow anything so full of life to exist."

Ichar felt enraged. "That's not true! You don't understand. I cannot stand by and have you say all this about Centrex. Computons are noble. They give their lives to duty. They maintain control that the world may live in peace." He felt his head spinning. "Michaal, you people are all crazy!"

"Ichar." Michaal's voice was soft, beseeching. "We opened our world to you. Let it in. Reach out, touch it, taste it. 'Your house is so beautiful' – your words, Icharitas." The voice was full with power, compassion. "You, all of mankind, can choose to live in this place."

Ichar squirmed away. "You came looking for me? Why, Michaal? Why, if the other world means so little to you? It's because you need me...." Suddenly the pieces fell together. "That's it! I've got it! You need me! I've got something you want! Admit it, Michaal – I have power. Centrex has total control...and you want it."

Michaal looked at him with sadness. "My heart fills with heaviness when you draw back."

Ichar held his breath. "I've got something you want, and I'm not going to give it to you." He had Michaal now. He glared across at him, cold, defiant.

Michaal continued to gaze at him gently. Ichar shifted his stance. Michaal remained looking at him. Ichar couldn't pull his eyes away. Finally, the guardian spoke.

"Yes, I do need you. There is something I would ask of you. Part of the plan is – "

"Stop. Don't go any further. I don't want to know."

"But you came in search, noble warrior – "

"Stop this nonsense."

" – in search of life, Icharitas. That's why you came – to find yourself. You have such courage."

"Who am I to you? Who, really?" Ichar felt crazy. "I think I'm just a part of your plan. Just something that fits into your scheme. Tell me!"

"I see in you what you refuse to see – courage, magnificence, strength. You are a giver of life, a lover of life."

"Stop!" Ichar turned away and leaned on the railing.

"Your world is suffering. It is dying. None of us would stand by and see the earth destroyed. Yet I am bound here, a prisoner of your disbelief. Without your consent, I cannot walk the earth."

"That's it!" said Ichar. "You just want to return to earth. It has nothing to do with me."

"I would not have you fail."

"But why me?" Ichar insisted stubbornly.

"Just for a moment, close your eyes."

Ichar closed his eyes and felt Michaal's hands reach into his heart. Slowly the fingers massaged the hardness of his heart until an warm glow filled his being. Michaal's words entered him. "Do you think that in that other place I was not with you? You must remember."

Michaal's words softened his heart. A promise long forgotten rose to his memory.

He remembered his vision of children, wandering in a garden of warmth and tenderness. A host of children looked at him; their eyes were innocent, and life shone radiant on their brows. He remembered his promise to the woman. These would be the fruit of his seed, these eloquent children of the future.

"I saw how you looked at them; I saw how your heart melted. That is what love is, Icharitas. You know you have loved. Have I not the same right? Can I not love you?"

Ichar reached out and touched Michaal's face. "Michaal, help me."

"I will, Icharitas. I will."

Chapter Six

Pamela awoke in the early afternoon to the sweet smell of rain. She sighed, contented, and fell back into a relaxed slumber. When she reawoke, the day was late. She sat up and stretched. When she hugged herself, she could feel her leanness. *I must have slept for ages*, she thought. *I'm absolutely famished.*

She paused and listened; someone was coming. The footsteps stopped at the door. A voice older than the hills began to speak outside.

"Mary who art in heaven, hail fruit of thy womb. Pray for us now and at the time of our deliverance."

My God! she thought to herself. *It's the old woman.*

Pamela came to the door and looked out. The old woman was full with age, gray hair loose and tangled, eyes dark and alive.

"I've come with fresh bread."

Pamela hesitated; she felt weak, unsure.

"Stop gawking like a girl who's lost her tongue and invite me into your house. I'm faint with the climb."

"It isn't much really, but come in." Pamela caught herself smoothing her smock and laughed. "Of course, you are most welcome. Enter my house, finest of the women of old Ireland."

"Thank you for your courtesy, Pamela Mary Duggan." The old woman lifted her skirts, ascended the step and crossed the threshold. "You've been living in filth, you have. You're worse than that mother of yours."

"You can just turn around and march right out again, bread and all, if you're going to be so snippy." Pamela leaned against the sill, amused at her outburst. She continued in a quieter voice, "And who, in God's name, might you be, so well acquainted with myself."

"Sit down and rest. I'll get you a little water for your bread." The old woman broke off part of the loaf and gave it to her. "It was I who gave you your name. I'm your godmother."

"My what?" But it was hard for Pamela to concentrate on anything but the sweetness of the bread. It was the first food she had eaten in weeks and she chewed it slowly. She sipped at the water and felt refreshed. When she had finished, she sat like a child, so overwhelmed was she by this wrinkled face that looked down at her with such an unfamiliar expression.

"You have fine cheekbones, Pamela Mary. But your hair needs some attention. You've been turned inside out now, haven't you?"

Pamela sat still, listening. She watched with amazement as the old woman took out an ivory comb from the basket she carried and started to comb at her tangles. Pamela's first impulse was to push her away, but there was such a gentleness about the crone that she relaxed and gave way to the pulling and tugging of the ivory comb. "Your hair's nothing but tangles," the old woman remarked. "It's been a hard coming for you, I can see."

"Stop pulling so hard," Pamela complained, but she smiled as she spoke. Gradually the tangles gave way and the combing moved to long sweeping motions. Pamela settled and, humming, allowed herself to be groomed for the first time in her adult life.

"What do you mean – my godmother?" she finally asked.

"It was at the time of your baptism. I was sitting in the back of the church, feeling unhappy because my womb had dried up and I felt barren and empty. I tell you, child, I was in a fine state that day. Then Monsignor Kirby came in the vestibule door and started setting up for a christening.

"I watched him, seeing the foolishness about the man – so empty of any love for his fellows, and him getting ready to baptize. I thought, the Lord works in strange ways. Then in comes your mother, and you all in a bundle and crying like it was the devil himself in you afraid for his life. But your mother had not been able to find a soul to stand up for you. Kirby got himself upset and told your mother to come back when she had found a godmother for the child. Foolish man!

"I tell you the grace of God put me in that church that day. I spoke up right boldly, and they both looked at me like I was the crazy one. And so, Pamela Mary, I held you in my arms when the priest put the salt on your tongue. And it was my voice that renounced Lucifer and all his pomp for you, and you became a child of God. And it was I that chose Mary for you. Mary, the Magdalena. It was her spirit I saw about you that day."

The old woman held Pamela's face in her palms. "There now, child, you look lovely as the spring."

Pamela felt the softness of her hands, velvety as chamois; tears welled in her eyes.

"You've had a hard time of it, I can see that."

"How did you find me?" Pamela asked.

"I just found myself walking up through the town and seeing the chapel on the hill. I decided to walk up to it and say the rosary for you, Pamela. And then I found you here."

"What's your name?" Pamela asked sleepily.

"Maia."

Pamela sighed and nodded, and the old woman gathered her in and rocked her gently to sleep.

She awoke to find herself in bed, a blanket tucked around her. The musky scent of a peat fire brought back memories of childhood. In the corner she could see cups set properly on saucers, and bread and some eggs. She felt hungry again.

She lay listening to the bubbling purr of the kettle boiling and to the faint hum from the porch. Every now and again she caught a bit of Gaelic song. Pamela felt like running out and hugging this old woman. She imagined the weeks ahead: her hunger would be satisfied; she would wake, still and lazy. She ran her fingers through her hair. Tomorrow she might even wash it.

Suddenly she felt a shiver of panic. Perhaps this was all a dream. "Maia," she called out softly.

"Yes, child, I'm right here. Are you ready for tea?"

"Yes, I'd love some." *It's true, this all really is true,* she thought to herself as she got up. Her world was alive, no longer filled with corpses and dead eyes.

Over the next few weeks, Maia washed and combed her, and nursed her strength back. Every morning, the old woman went down to the village at the base of the hill; each noon she returned with her hamper full. Pamela felt her flesh filling, her skin waxing soft.

It was on these summer days that she explored the hills along the coast. One morning, as she began to stroll through the valley behind the chapel, she was caught by a raft of dark clouds that came scudding down the coast. She ran along a path that led into a ravine. She stopped under a large tree and sat out the downpour.

When the sun returned, Pamela remained gazing at the green around her. Unlike the surrounding countryside, the ravine had not been burned brown by the long summer. She watched as a woodcock landed in front of her and started to push among the moist leaves. He twitched a tail feather as though he had an itch. He found two grubs under an old leaf, took them in his beak and flew off. She leaned back against the tree's rough bark.

The circular web of a spider caught her eye as it glistened with raindrops; it looked like a brilliant crystal suspended in space. Pamela sat enthralled by the enchanted weave of it.

She looked farther up and observed the branches over her; the leaves hung, heavy with rain. It was a hazel tree she was sitting under. She remembered that when she had been a little girl, she had watched a dowser search for water with a forked hazel stick.

She stood up and stretched, feeling beneath her the roots of the tree surging out into the earth. The earth itself was alive. She sensed its longing to articulate its travail, its yearning to draw itself forward into consciousness. She felt oneness with the earth, became one with the upward yearning of the tree, the thin sunward reaching of the grass.

She spun about. The sun warmed her face. She felt eagerness, expectancy, all about her. One with the earth and all that moved upon it, she laughed and sang old lullabies. She could feel the life stirring in her womb. How she longed for this new life she carried to come into the world. She could hardly wait to see her baby. She knew it would be a beautiful child, the most beautiful child in the whole county. Slowly she wended her way homeward, full of impatience and expectation.

That evening she had a talk with the old woman. Long into the night the two sat in front of the fire. Finally Maia said, "The Feast of Saint Michael the Archangel is not far off. He was the warrior who fought against the darkness, who sent Lucifer into the pit."

"Well?"

"There's still another step to be taken. Something more is needed – an event beyond the sword or the cross. Maybe an embrace?"

Confused, Pamela got up and went outside. The sky was thick with cloud; she couldn't see the stars. She found herself thinking of Richard. In her heart she held a hope she dared not speak.

One day Maia returned from town with a length of unbleached cloth. "It's for you," she announced. "You need a smock. The weather will become cold before long, and the wind will be raw. You'll need something warmer to wear."

"Where did you get this? And where does all our food come from? Tell me."

"It's given. The people in the town know you're here, but they want nothing to do with you. They think you might be a witch, but they don't want you on their consciences, either. It suits them fine to have me, the crazy woman, looking after you." She smiled. "And there are some who see you differently. You are not without grace. Besides," the old woman continued, "it's good that they should give. It's the poor such as we who draw out their kindness." The old woman's eyes were dark and bottomless; her face was creased with lines and wrinkles, like land resting after harvest.

"I'm no dressmaker, Maia. I don't know the first thing about sewing."

"Of course you don't. Well, Pamela Mary, you begin by laying it out on the floor." The two of them started the cutting on their hands and knees.

When Pamela walked the beach in her homespun smock,

word spread among the townspeople. A few fishermen told the story of seeing a woman in a whitish smock and a blue shawl, her hair long and auburn. When they saw her walking along the rocky shingle, the fishermen out in their small curraghs blessed themselves – not because they feared her as a witch, but because they feared the hope that was stirring in their own hearts.

As the days grew shorter, Pamela began to carry herself with a certain straightness that seemed to start in her legs and go up through her back to her head. The child in her womb extended her stomach, but it didn't sway her back. She almost felt as if her being was mantled with a soft aura of light.

One morning, when Maia was preparing for her daily trip to the village, Pamela surprised herself.

"I want to go to the village with you."

"It would do you no harm at all," Maia replied.

Arm in arm, the two of them set off for Enniscrone. They entered the village from the back, and walked up a lane toward the sea. The main street consisted of docks and beached boats on one side, storm-blasted storefronts on the other. Pamela left the old woman at the bakery and went on to enjoy the displays in the shop windows. Few people were about, but those who were stopped and stared with expressions of curiosity. Pamela guessed from their manner that Centrex had not bothered to claim this bleak outpost.

At one point a dog ran toward her, barking. His owner called him back and scolded him, but Pamela knew the dog's bark had been one of welcome. She called out to him kindly to let him know he had been understood.

After admiring some wool sweaters in a shop window, Pamela went in to look at the yarn. A woman with a pinched face appeared from the back of the store. For a moment the two women stared at one another. The storekeeper seemed confused.

Pamela smiled politely, unsure what to do. She started to look through the bins, testing the wool. She knew the woman was watching her. She could hear shoes behind the counter shuffling awkwardly. The woman must know she did not have any money; she probably wanted to throw her out. Pamela became afraid to stay any longer.

Outside, she felt better. She realized she had almost asked for the wool. She shivered, embarrassed at the thought. She would accept no charity. She did have her pride. She marched off to find Maia in the bakery. Pamela waited until they were outside, beyond earshot of the plump rosy man behind the counter. Then she spoke.

"It's time we stopped begging for our bread," she began. "It's a disgrace. I will not be given to like a poor servant girl."

The loaf of bread breaking across her shoulders stopped her. "You listen here." The old woman's eyes blazed as she hit Pamela again with the bread. "The Virgin wasn't so proud she couldn't accept an inn stable. And who are you? Jesus himself begged his bread. You, young lady, have a lot to learn."

She took Pamela's arm and they started back. "How else

do you expect these people to earn their way to heaven?" Maia answered her own question, "By giving alms to the poor. And we are the poor – don't you ever forget it. We are saved by the love we give them in return. You acting so high and mighty – you aren't even worth the gift of that wool."

The storekeeper's pinched face came back to Pamela. That was what she had run from. The woman hadn't wanted to push her out; she had wanted to give to her. Pamela looked back down the street. A few people were staring after them. She felt she'd not known herself until this moment. "Next time," Pamela said to herself, "it will be different."

That evening, as they were putting the food on the table, the old woman made an announcement. "I've found a place near the sea where I would like to keep the vigil."

Pamela looked at her in amazement.

"Next week is the time when day and night are of equal length. We celebrated the feast day of Michaelmas long before the coming of Saint Patrick. Next week, we shall celebrate it again."

Pamela felt afraid. "When will it be?"

"Soon. But don't worry, I'll tell you. You kept the Midsummer vigil with me in June, near Kinvarra."

"Why didn't you mention it?" Pamela asked, amazed that Maia had known all along.

"There didn't seem the need. You see, I felt troubled that night, but I didn't know what God wanted, so I went to walk beside the sea. When I returned, there you were on my vigil rock. So I sat nearby in the shadows and watched with you until morning."

"You were there with me the whole time? When I was sitting on that rock I had the strangest feeling, as if the earth itself waited and watched with me."

"And so it did indeed. There are certain rocks that are sacred, child. At one time I used to believe Saint Patrick himself had stood on them, but I know now they must have been blessed by the angels long before he ever came to Ireland. My mother showed them to me when I was a girl. The gypsies use them, too. Some call them womb-rocks, because when the sea comes into them, into the great hollows underneath, they vibrate with the waves. On the days of equal day and night it is said that man and woman stand equal, one within the other."

Who was this woman who was calling her forth into the ancient rites? Pamela wondered again at the accident of their meeting.

One day, Pamela awoke craving wool the way she had recently been craving certain foods. She decided that this was the day to visit the wool lady. *But how will I repay her kindness?* she wondered. Slowly, like a long-forgotten memory, a dream image arose. On the back of her closed eyelids she could see a blue-white pearl, soft and full as the earth itself. She watched it float in her vision, exquisitely beautiful. The thought of the pearl somehow gave her courage. She had a baby growing within her; in a few months it would have to be clothed. For this, she had to have wool.

"I'm going to the village," she announced to Maia. She headed down the hill, eager as a girl.

117

The tinkling of the bell above the door brought the store-keeper from the back room. The village woman hesitated, then moved forward, awkward, uncertain. She was not as old as Pamela had thought; she could have been an older sister.

"Hello," Pamela began. "Would you help me? I need some wool and a set of knitting needles. I am expecting soon and my baby will need clothing." She paused. "You know I have no money."

Pamela looked across the counter into the frightened eyes; in them she could see a land of untold wealth and riches, a place of love beyond measure. Pamela invited her forward. This woman would be blessed the rest of her days.

The woman gestured to the corner of the store.

"Take what you need from that bin over there. It's soft and won't scratch. You'll need small-gauge needles. I'll find some for you."

"You are blessed. Thank you."

"My name is Lillian. There is talk of you hereabouts."

"I'm from Galway. It's here I will have the child."

"A blessing it will be upon all of us." Lillian wrapped up the wool and needles and handed them to Pamela. "Come again."

Outside, Pamela stood in amazement. Her heart pounded and elation ran through her. It was not that she'd been given what she had asked for that astounded her. It was that she had been able to transform a frightened, pinched little woman into a different being altogether. There was something she could not comprehend wakening within her. She could feel her heart opening. A power mightier than the sword or the cross was growing within her. But she kept silent in her heart. Her time had not yet come.

That night, she told Maia everything that had gone on in the wool shop. When she finished, Maia looked at her for a long time. Pamela met her gaze. "You needn't be walking the roads anymore," she said finally. "You know you can rest here with me."

Maia nodded. "I've found my place. Yet there's still one task that awaits me."

"What is it?"

The old woman settled closer to the small fireplace. "My bones have been aching and weary lately. The fall is not far off, and then the winter." She looked about the cottage. "This, in the winter, is no place for a child to come into the world."

"I've been thinking that myself. And yet I feel tied here." Pamela paused. "In fact, God himself couldn't get me to leave." She was surprised at her stubbornness.

"Well, we'll see. This ache in my bones is worse than anything I've felt before." Maia sat, trying to solve the puzzle. "There's something about this place that puts the ache in me, but it is still too early to tell what it is."

"What do you think it is?" asked Pamela.

"It concerns you, but the nature of it is not yet clear." Maia looked at her. "It's been so hard, Pamela, so hard. I've walked down every road and walkway of all of Ireland. But I've been a faithful woman. I've never given up the trust."

After a pause, Maia continued drowsily, "I remember once

seeing a gypsy woman nurse an urchin boy who had been standing by, watching her nurse her own child. When he first saw her, he swore at her, but she touched him and brought him to her body, and he softened and sucked."

Pamela wondered what to say.

"I have seen too many urchin men in my day." Maia seemed to sink into memories.

Who was Maia? Pamela wondered. Where had she come from? How had she earned her way? Had she been that gypsy mother?

For a while the two drifted on their thoughts. Then Pamela turned and considered the roundness of her own body, which felt firm, full with life. She ran her hands over her extended stomach; she felt like a bulb about to burst into flower. She thought of Richard. She wondered if they would ever meet again.

She remembered a story from childhood. A saint met a leper man on the road. The saint had gone up to the leper and embraced him, kissed him on the lips. She couldn't remember how the story had ended, for some reason, but it had always haunted her. To kiss a leper...she could practically smell the rotting flesh. She shivered at the thought of such an embrace, wondered why the saint had done it.

"Maia, do you know that story about the saint and the leper?"

"Of course. Doesn't everyone? The saint kisses the leper child on the lips and the leper turns into the Christ child. Why?"

"Just wondering."

"Pamela, tomorrow night is the fall equinox, the Eve of Michaelmas. We will do a vigil that you'll have a safe delivery. You'd best get some sleep." The old woman reached out and took her hand for a moment. Then they both went to bed.

The two women sat side by side, watching the moon rise across the sea. The old woman seemed to have become one with the stone, a part of the large rounded rock that fell to the sea far below. The surf reverberated against the hollow recesses in the cliff. This thundering drowned out any possibility of shared speech. Beneath Pamela, the rock shook; salty mist fell upon her cheeks and eyelids from above.

Then the old woman started. Swaying slowly, she began to recite the rosary. Her chant cut across the waves' thunder.

"Hail Mary, who art in heaven, hallowed be thy name. Blessed is the fruit of thy womb."

Pamela answered in a shout. "Pray for us now, and at the time of our deliverance. Amen."

On through the rosary, hour after hour, their voices rose above the thunder, at times silenced by the sea, at other times taken up by the roar, until the sea itself prayed with them. On they chanted, at one with the sea, at one with the surging waters.

"Holy Mary, Mother of God."

"*Ora pro nobis.*"

"Mary, Refuge of Sinners."

"*Ora pro nobis.*"

"Mary, Mother of Life."

"*Ora pro nobis.*"

"Mary Magdalena, Lover of Men."

"Pray for us."

The two of them faded into the soft fold of the rock. Pamela became aware that the mass of stone they both sat upon was warming her. Coming up from the stone were currents she had never felt before.

Her body swayed like a tree as the wind blew against her. Her chanting became soundless; her body trembled like a harpstring in the wind. On and on the two of them sang.

Joy rose into her fibers. Joy rose upward and opened in her, bright, shining, like the sound of the sea itself. A glow rose, expanded in her like the tide. Wider and wider she became, a home for all sound. The sea flowed into her womb and out. She felt like a vessel, a cradle for all that was living, for all the world. She marveled at what she had been given to contain.

She could feel her eyes glisten, her heart fill to bursting. Her mystery had unfolded. Her dowry was the earth itself. *Who would have believed such wealth lay hidden*, she thought, amazed. Her voice fell to a note of contentment, a single note. At one with what dwelled within the sea, at one with what dwelled within the earth, she felt radiant with fecundity.

"Hail, woman full of grace," the old woman greeted her. "Blessed art thou on earth as in heaven. Blessed is the fruit of thy womb."

Dawn washed the sky. Pamela swam in bliss, closed her

eyes, resonated with the grace of the sea, felt life trembling within her. She felt exalted. For now and for always, she had riches beyond compare.

With the morning sun, the two women gathered their things and headed up the hill, serene. Pamela looked back and noticed how green the moss shone on their rock; how fine the mist was as it drifted across it. The sea tossed and glinted beyond the rock's edge. A wave of joy drenched her; she held back a sob. Finally, she knew herself: the life bearer.

She thought of the sailor far out at sea. Had her embrace no limit?

Chapter Seven

"You never had a mother, Ichar." The words entered him like a silvered scalpel. "You clutched at an empty dream." Michaal's voice softened, but cut clean. "No one can give you the mother you never had. And yet in your heart you long for her. Out with it." Again Michaal's voice was gentle.

Had he substituted a make believe? A lie that seemed easier than the truth? Anguish pulled at his chest.

"You forced yourself to forget that helpless longing. You buried yourself in despair. It was you who chose to treat yourself this way. Let it go." Michaal's voice was like a physical touch.

Ichar wept. He had wanted to disown this lost creature within him, but this child of his past clung, pulled at him, made him face his pain. He remembered a small, battered velveteen bear his father had given him. The times he had clutched it to him! The times he had hidden it from view under the sheets! He remembered the morning they had discovered it and taken it away for no reason at all. The tantrum came forward and racked his body. He shook with infantile anger. They had taken away his bear, his one possession. Then, after the anger, he felt something he had never experienced before, a longing for what he'd never had.

"Let it come. Out with it, dear friend. You never felt the warmth of a mother's hand, the soft feel of a mother's breast. The lullaby of your mother singing, the gentle touch of her fingers on your furry head, the sweetness of her milk. You never knew your mother's heart close to yours. You never knew such love. This is the wordless longing of your heart. Grieve, my friend, for the mother you never had, the child you never were."

Ichar gave himself over to tears, felt them running down his face, warm and cleansing. He wailed, at one with the motherless. For an instant he saw himself abandoned in a sterile pit of his own waste, an unwanted child left behind in the dark. Gradually, the hurt melted into peace. The wound had been lanced and through it, raw and open, he saw that other part of him that lived beyond any hope of redemption. He opened his eyes, and there was Michaal standing like an older brother in front of him. The healing had begun.

He began to remember fragments of his youth. Yet always in his mind was the fact that they had taken from him the only thing of any importance – that ragged, weary piece of velveteen he had known only as "bear".

At times, spite would come up, sour like bile, and he would practically choke. At other times, he had strange flashes that he was being watched. It was never anything specific – just sometimes, for moments, it was as if his companions were really people behind mirrors, scheming. Didn't they keep talking about some plan? He wanted to question everything, but all he could do was subdue this wordless spite that had come up from his past.

Apart from these moments, in the days that followed, Ichar felt he was living a childhood he never had before. He felt free in a way he had never been, released into a sunlit world where everything was new and young.

One day, Michaal had taken him to the sea. Michaal walked with him into the water, held him gently on the surface and splashed water over him.

"That's it. I've got you."

Richard was aware of being moved by Michaal, forward and back, in the water. He felt his body lighten. He became aware of the sun, warm on his face. He tried to trust, yet he knew he would sink.

"Relax! You think too much. I'm not going to let you sink."

Ichar became aware he was actually floating. Tentatively, he let himself feel pleasure. He felt Michaal's hands beneath him, holding him afloat. He could lay there forever. He let himself go. He relaxed, secure in those arms.

"You're floating by yourself now. You don't need me to hold you up."

Ichar felt the hands letting him go. He discovered that he remained afloat. He could do it himself.

"See how easy it is!"

Ichar felt himself flooded with affection for this man.

Suddenly he felt himself sinking, sputtered saltwater from his mouth, saw the cliffs falling into the sea. He ran shivering back onto the hot sand.

He sat on the beach, pushing his heels into the sand, pushing down a craziness inside him. He longed to have this man for himself alone.

His friend came out of the water and sat down beside him. "It takes a little getting used to, but floating is just a simple matter of trusting yourself. You'll always come to the top. When you know that, you'll be ready to learn how to swim." Michaal smiled, lay back, closed his eyes.

Ichar wanted to tell him that he in no way trusted himself. In the silence, he became absorbed with Michaal. Crazily, he wanted to cry out and ask this man to hold him. He pushed his hands deep into the sand, frightened of what he felt. "Michaal," he called softly.

Michaal opened one eye, squinted against the sun, pushed himself up on one elbow. He surveyed the anguish on Ichar's face. "Sometimes I just don't understand you." He smiled at Ichar. "Come on. Let's get dressed."

Ichar dressed. This man could love him without the same need he felt to possess.

They were just coming in sight of the Phoenix when he noticed a figure waving from the patio. Michaal waved back and broke into a run. Ichar watched as he lifted the woman up into a joyful embrace. He remembered being touched by this woman, the night of the feast. He studied her now, noticing her round hips, her flat stomach that arched ever so slightly upward. He noted, too, her breasts, her sculptured neck that spoke of royalty, her laughing face. For an instant he thought he was looking at Pamela.

"Hello." She smiled. "You have the same eyes as Michaal." She took his hand.

"I'd like you to meet Delana Meropa, Daughter of the Sea." Michaal gestured elegantly and the woman burst into laughter.

"Tomorrow he'll christen me Stella, Princess of the Stars. Yesterday I was Demeter. Once I was Eve." Her laughter flowed like water. "And always I am the same woman."

The feeling Ichar had on the beach burst upon him in full force. He felt hungry to hold her in his arms, to kiss her lips, to make her his. To possess her. She was so beautiful! He felt an overpowering urge to take her; yet at the same time felt inferior, like an urchin in the presence of royalty.

"I have a present for you." She straightened his hair with her hand and put on his head a crown of gardenias. The heavy perfume tumbled down. She embraced him. For an instant he thought he would suffocate. It was all too much. Her embrace was too close, her warmth too frightening.

"Forgive me," said Delana. As she spoke, she stepped back.

"The scent is so powerful," Ichar apologized. She was so close, so soft. If she had come any closer, he felt he would have been changed forever.

He saw her often after that. Once, he and Delana talked together in the square. It was a little after sunset, before the stars come out. Delana had been very quiet. He was torn between a feeling of being brother to this woman and a desire to run off with her. She was the embodiment of dreams he had never before allowed himself to have. He felt a crushing love for her that made him frightened.

"You have changed since you came. There is no longer a grayness about you. You have grown strong and happy."

He sensed a question coming.

"What is that around your neck?" she asked.

"It is the seven stars of the constellation called the Big Dipper. It was given to me when I was very young. But then it was lost...." He waved his hand. "The way it was lost is a long story, but it did return, and in a very strange manner." Once, back when he and Mel had been as close as twin brothers, in a time before he had been rejected by the computon elite, Mel had come up to him. He remembered how shocked he had been when Mel had handed him the box.

"I found it in my mailbox last night. When I saw it, I realized the mistake – such a beautiful thing as this would never have come to me." There'd been a tone of such aggrieved bitterness in Mel's voice. "Apparently there's some compu-boob out there who's convinced I'm you."

Ichar had thought afterward that the first coldness between himself and Mel could be traced to that evening. He turned to Delana and told her as much as he dared. "It was given by my father. I lost it and in a strange way it was returned to me by...a friend."

She looked at it carefully, nodded as though it confirmed something she had been thinking. "We call your constellation "The Bear," but I like your name for it better."

Ichar touched the pendant around his neck. "Sometimes

this pattern shapes itself in my mind's eye as a chalice." He paused, searching for words. "I've often felt these seven stars hang about my neck as some kind of promise of what's yet to be."

"My constellation is the Pleiades," said Delana. "There is a guardian who watches over the women of this constellation. His name is Orion."

They sat quietly together as the sky overhead darkened into night. Out of the silence she spoke.

"The last days of a great age are coming to a close, and this will bring a great opportunity. Your race could stand free of its past, like a newborn child." She touched his hand gently. "You can do it."

"You make it sound so easy." They rose and strolled along the promenade. She took his arm. Ichar stopped her. "Delana, what does it all mean? Tell me simply."

She spoke slowly. "Your task will be to embody this dark power. In some way, beyond reason – deeper than thinking mind can fathom – you will stand one with the force of evil. And then, with that one gift given to your kind, the gift of choice – and in your frailty – you will choose."

"And what about you in all this?" Ichar asked.

"I do not know what part I will be called to play. Sometimes I think it will have to do with some kind of rescue."

Suddenly, for no reason he could remember, he started to tell her a story Pamela had once told him. "Once upon a time a woman was dragged off into the underworld. There she was trapped until a goddess journeyed down into the darkness to find her."

They strolled along in a thoughtful silence. Then Delana stopped and kissed him gently on the cheek. "Thank you," she said softly.

A few days after he had walked with Delana, he went with Iden to explore the castle. They hiked back along the top of the ridge, across a plowed field full of seagulls. Stopping, they took off their sandals and chased the gulls in their bare feet. Then they walked the warm furrows like young boys. After that, they met some women picking strawberries. They accompanied them back to help bake sweet bread, over which they poured the fruit.

One day, he and Iden collected honey. Ichar found it hard to believe even when he saw it with his own eyes. Tiny creatures swarmed and buzzed over large flat slabs. Iden told him again how bees took nectar from the flowers, and in return, the flowers used the bees to fertilize their seeds. Iden broke off a piece of honeycomb. Ichar had eaten honey for breakfast, but honeycomb was even more delicious. He asked for another piece.

One day, he ran through the fields, in and out through the orchard, racing among the huge cashew trees that grew beside the fields. He deliberately lost himself, then hid in a field of corn, walked back through the rows, looked up at their tasseled tops. He laughed as he shook the huge stalks, watched the powdery pollen fall over the forming cobs, over himself. He ran his hand over the growing ears and told himself they'd soon be ready. He felt like stealing an armful. Then he came out into a field of unfamiliar-looking plants –

huge circular mounds of twining leaves. He approached the plants cautiously, pushed aside the giant flat leaves. There, hidden in the shade, were huge warty lumps fastened to the vines. He was struck by their size. Some of the lumps were so large he couldn't encircle them with his arms.

He told Michaal and Delana about his discovery that evening. Michaal laughed. "They're called squash," Michaal told him. The three of them talked into the night, of the garden, of growing plants. Ichar learned that in order for some squash to ripen, they must first be cut off the vine.

Several mornings he went out with Tommy and lowered the nets with him, helped him throw back all but the very largest of fish. Then they moved on and reset the nets for the smallest of fish, anchovies, and caught them in uncountable numbers. When he returned, he was giddy with the sea and his knowledge of what swam within it. He stood beside Tommy, shouting at the landlubbers to hurry and fasten the lines and not to ask so many questions.

There was so much to take in, so many questions to ask. Ichar wondered if these beings ever slept. He watched at nightfall as a group headed off to an old church on the hillside. He wondered what they did there. He wondered, too, when he would be ready to really share in their work. He felt like a boy watching his elders, anxious to be grown-up.

Then, one day, Michaal and Delana were no longer there. He felt at a loss. There was no one he could just be with. Iden's idea of playing in the square or exploring the fields no longer interested him. He looked at his nude body in the mirror, stood up and paraded himself. He was deeply tanned, broad shouldered. He admired his penis, twisted his body, looked at his back. The gauntness had disappeared. He felt straighter, taller. He liked what he saw, smiled at his image, saw for the first time the beauty in his own face.

Tomorrow, he decided, he would join the workers.

The workshop was full of dust and noise. Ichar wondered when the buzzing would stop. Beside him, two men sent wood through a saw. A burly man stood right beside the whirling blade. Ichar had never imagined it would be like this.

"Hey, you, how about a hand with the unloading?"

Someone seemed to need help. He hopped off the bench and joined a group of men.

"Well, Ichar, what do you think?" David came around the corner and winked at him.

Before he could answer, David had put his shoulder under a large timber. "Get the other end, Ic." He turned to the third man. "Dominic, where do you want it?"

Ichar liked the way David shortened his name. It seemed a long time ago now since he'd met David on that faraway hillside.

Ichar heaved. Wood wasn't as heavy as he had expected. They edged past some men completing a wall, eased the timber onto a rack and backed out of the way of another team. Ichar hung back to pull a sliver out of his hand.

"Here, take these until your hands harden." David pulled some leather gloves from his belt. "Timber is hard on soft hands."

Ichar took his time putting them on and then, wiping the sweat off his forehead, headed back for the next piece of timber. He saw that David had stopped to talk to the man who was directing things, a man called Cristo. Ichar waited. He watched the men hoist timbers. Their arms were so large, their muscles thick and rippling. He fell back before a crew of men carrying away enormous bundles of roofing slats.

David stood beside him, then pulled him aside.

"Hot? Take off your shirt. Now stand back and look at what you see. There's a lot of men moving about, right? A wall is going up, wood is being stacked, boat ribs, tables, beds are being built. We need many things." David smiled at him. "Don't worry if it doesn't make a lot of sense. You've got to remember that you've just started."

Then it was lunch. Ichar looked up. Machines had stopped; men were dusting themselves off.

"You've done a good job, Ic." David reached over to grasp his hand.

"It was fun." He brushed wood chips off himself, looked about at the machines. The men moved toward the door. They didn't have to work like this, Richard decided. Men didn't work like this unless someone drove them. There was a secret here. What did they know here that Centrex didn't?

David was waiting for him. There was always someone hounding him; he suddenly felt irritated, angry.

After lunch, Ichar felt no better. He sent his excuses to David through a man he didn't know, then went back to his room and slept the whole afternoon. He woke with a headache. He wished Michaal were back. He got up and went out into the square and saw Orgen sketching the fountain basin with its vacant plinth.

Orgen was one of the people who went up into the hills in the evenings to work nights in the ancient church looking eastward over the countryside. "You can come up and work there yourself if you want. Come with me tonight and I'll show you what I'm doing."

That evening, Ichar found that the church was merely a silhouette, a ruined shell of the building it once had been. Overhead, up through the rotting beams, he could see the evening sky. He noticed the grouping of seven stars.

"You can see the Bear early tonight. That's a good sign," Orgen remarked, pointing.

Within the confines of the walls worked the artists. Against the walls in careful piles or cluttered heaps was work put aside. Here and there were fragments of objects that had been found around the ruins. He looked at the works in progress, talked to the few who seemed willing to converse.

Orgen became involved in a cube of flowing colors. After a while Ichar began to watch a quiet old man chisel away at a tall figurine. A winged creature seemed to be emerging from the wood. The arc lights were turned higher as evening moved toward midnight. Ichar wanted to ask questions, but the man's eyes were only for his work. It was as if he was on another plane, struggling with something beyond Ichar's knowledge. His hands' meticulous movements – his commitment to the truth of the wood – seemed to anchor him, while his spirit fought elsewhere.

Ichar watched the wood taking form beneath the man's hands. When it was finished, he knew it would give forth, like perfume, the essence of the man's struggle, all his courage and dignity. When it was finished, there would be an aura about it that would make people refer to it as "beautiful." It would remain a signpost for those coming after.

"You do understand." The old man's voice brought him out of his trance.

Ichar nodded.

"Yet you don't speak. Never mind. That is the beginning of wisdom." He put his arm around Ichar's shoulder. "Come outside, Ichar." The old man repeated his name several times. "We are not altogether strangers, you and I. No, I think not."

They sat at the far end of the ancient columned portico. The old man continued, "Long ago, the story goes, a youth by your name – Icarus – he tried to fly to the sun...."

"He flew too close. The wax in his wings melted and he plunged back to earth," Ichar finished for him.

"When we get close..." The old man broke off, musing. "When you ran from work yesterday – it was fear of your power, yes? Of your pleasure?"

Ichar sat silently.

"When we get close to that for which we long..." The old man began again. "And you are close now..." He lifted his voice. "Beware!"

Ichar jumped a little.

"When the boy takes his first step into manhood, it is a time of great danger."

Ichar stood and looked down at this man, sitting on the stoop. Was he trying to frighten him?

The old man patted the stone beside him. "Don't run off. Sit down again."

Ichar took his place and the old man continued. "In a way it was a test for the boy. The truth is in the wax – in his own frailty. The young man had to prove he could be trusted with his wings...but the sun proved too alluring. He couldn't just fly near it. No, he had to possess it all for himself." The old man heaved a sigh of great weariness. "It is forever the way."

"But Icarus needed to have wings." Ichar corrected the old man. "Can't you imagine the moment of flying? That moment when man can rise off the earth? To soar upward into the heavens – there is not a person alive who has not dreamed of that. I would want not to be earthbound, but to fly up to the stars."

"True, true. We all want to fly. But that is not the way to reach the stars. Did you know that? Let me tell you! Icarus's father built a great maze, for he was the architect for the labyrinth at Crete. There inside the labyrinth was kept a monster."

For a moment Ichar saw his own father – the designer of Centrex. His hand moved instinctively to the seven-star amulet around his neck. He did not want to think about the monster inside.

"You want to fly? You must first enter the labyrinth, and

in the darkness, face the monster that awaits you." The old man waved a finger. "Only then will you be able to reach the stars. Only then will you not fall back to earth."

"But you must not kill the monster," he added. "That would make you its prisoner forever. You must find another way."

The two sat in silence, side by side, young and old. At last Ichar rose. The sky was beginning to lighten. He took the old man's hand in his, saw the lacework of blue veins across its back.

"Peace be with you, old man."

"My blessings go with you, young man." They bowed to each other. Ichar walked back down the road. He entered the square, stood looking at the empty plinth within the fountain.

People started to gather. David came up and greeted him.

"Ichar, yesterday was hard for you?"

"Today everything will be perfect." Ichar laughed.

"I finished the planing," he told him. "Today we chisel. We have to cap one end and slot the other."

"Cap, slot – what are you talking about?"

David laughed. "I'll show you. This piece we're crafting is going to be a work of art!" They walked up the hill path between the houses, accompanied by perhaps fifty others.

When they reached the workshop, they lifted a heavy piece of oak onto the bench. "I didn't tell you yesterday," David said. "You've probably guessed by now that this piece will be the bowsprit for Michaal's new vessel, down in the harbor."

"Oh," said Ichar vaguely. He suddenly found it hard to listen.

"This is the section we've been working on. It protrudes out over the bow. The cap is here, for the running line." David stopped and looked at him. "Are you listening?"

Ichar realized he was not paying attention.

"Here." His friend drew a diagram on the bench. "Here's the slot we have to cut." Ichar sensed something familiar in what he saw in front of him. Something from that other world that made him uneasy. David's diagram helped a little. He forced himself to concentrate.

The chipping away began. Ichar held the bowsprit tight until the soft skin of his hand burned, hot and tired. He took his turn with chisel and mallet, blew the flies away from his face, watched his sweat drop into the sawdust. Chisel, hold, rest. Repeat. Then the long sweep of the sanding block. Slowly his body softened and his grip relaxed. His joints became oiled and loose. Anxiety left him.

He found himself excited by the work. He knew they would finish the bowsprit today. He ignored the thoughts that were stirring in his memory. More urgent was the power he felt flowing through his muscles.

David laid out the tools; Ichar took them. They mounted the cap, bored the plugs. Ichar handed David the mallet. David slammed tight the cap. Together they lifted it end for end. Ichar could feel power surge through him, molding the wood. The work spun on.

Their saw hummed; men moved past them, in and out among the benches. The passing men smelled salty, spicy.

Ichar licked sweat from his lips. He felt beautiful, male, masculine, thick with hair, covered with sawdust. He and David were partners in a pulsing dance. On and on they worked into the afternoon, while the rhythm of the motions rang through his body.

He could go on forever. He pounded the hammer in rhythm with the blood pulsing in his head. "Work, David, work," Ichar chanted.

"Work!" David replied. "I love it."

Ichar suddenly knew one of life's deepest pleasures. "This is how you do it!" he shouted above the roar. This was how men shared their joy. Power surged through his body. He felt himself slipping into manhood. What was there to fear?

Then it was finished. Excited to see how it would look in place, they loaded the bowsprit on their shoulders and ran down the cobbled path into the square, past the empty fountain, out along the breakwater.

"Where to from here?" Ichar asked.

"Down, then to the left. You'll see the drydock as you round the retaining wall."

Ichar felt relief. The energy that had throbbed through his head all day was moving, breaking. He felt oddly tired.

He gripped the bowsprit less firmly. "I need a rest," he said.

"Not much farther now." David's own voice sounded strained. "Just around the end of the wall."

Suddenly, before them stood the vessel. The vessel! Ichar reeled to a stop. It stood there, new, pristine, just as he had remembered it: the white enameled hull, the exquisite lines.

There before his eyes was the model he had built, perfect in every detail. Only it was not a model, it was life-size, and it was real!

He could not keep the memory of that last night buried any longer. Images exploded, painful and red before him. Mel's mocking laughter filled his ears. He felt himself gripped by rage and pain.

He had gone back to his study, found the door open, had gone in. There, in the center of the blue broadloomed floor, were the remains of his model. It had been smashed into little pieces. That which had been so precious to him had been destroyed beyond all hope of repair.

A rage that had no boundaries, no understanding, rushed up through him. He dropped the bowsprit, shouted to everyone to get away and stationed himself on deck. He was no longer himself, flooded as he was by this dark fury. The vessel was his. He had made it. He would fight off anyone who came near. Split off from the world around him, he stood, seething blackness in a world of light. All else mattered not. The vessel had become everything.

Suddenly, out of nowhere, Michaal was walking toward him. Ichar saw him, then turned his back on him.

"What's happened? What's come over you?"

Ichar spoke with his back turned. "It's my bowsprit," he said. "It fits on my vessel."

"Yes, David told me you were done. You've made one little mistake, though." Michaal laughed kindly. "That vessel was built from *my* specifications."

Ichar turned and faced him defiantly. "It's mine!"

"It will carry us into a new world," Michaal continued. "I have designed it specially to take us forward. Trust me."

But Ichar didn't listen. Instead he was shouting, "It's mine! It's mine!" He tried to suppress the words before they came out. Even while he yelled, a part of him wanted to reach out, tell Michaal the horrible thing that had happened. But he couldn't control himself.

Michaal turned and walked a little distance away. Ichar stopped yelling. He pressed his lips together. He was afraid the rage would return and swallow him up. Suddenly he realized he had no control over this part of himself. He quieted down, paced back and forth in front of the vessel.

Michaal spoke very gently. "Come up to the Phoenix."

Ichar nodded. He longed to reach out, to ask for help, but he held himself back rigidly. He was afraid that if he relaxed his control, he might betray Michaal, betray this bright world. He looked at his feet. He felt guilty and ashamed. What had come over him?

As he fought to control himself, a voice pounded again and again in his head: "Smash him!" He couldn't believe that he wanted to hit Michaal. Michaal paced along calmly at his side. Ichar was possessed with a desire to kill him.

In silence, the two of them climbed the narrow stone steps to the Phoenix. Hospadar was there. Delana. Cristo. David. Ichar looked about, recognizing so many faces. He sat down. Ashamed, he stared at a pomegranate, hefted it, listened. What had gotten into him?

"How did it happen?" Delana began.

"David said it came over him just as they came in sight of the vessel. There is no explanation." Hospadar spoke.

"It must have been some chance occurrence," Cristo mused. "There is no use looking for explanations now. It has happened. The dark force has entered Fino. And it has entered through this man."

Michaal spoke. "I thought I understood him. It was necessary to let him find his own power. But he has now split off. His will is now controlled by another."

Everyone looked at Icharitas. He balanced the pomegranate in his hand and looked away.

"My concern is with the child. Will the child be safe?" Delana looked about for an answer.

"We had to leave the woman on her own," Alice, an elder, replied. "But she, too, needed to use her strength. Worry not. The child will be safe."

Ichar broke open the pomegranate, poked about at the seeds. A child. His mind idled over this new information. Everybody knew but him. They had hidden it from him. What else had they kept hidden from him?

"It is, indeed, serious." Ichar felt Alice's eyes on him as she talked. "We wanted a connection, but not like this. It is too much for him." She sounded anxious, concerned.

"There is always risk, with mankind, with free will. Always the risk that mankind will be swamped by that other voice," Delana said somberly.

Ichar felt numb with horror. Was he the one who would destroy it all? Was he to be the one? His stomach ached but he dared not speak. He sat sucking the seeds of the pomegranate. He could not help anyone. He knew now he was destined to be the betrayer.

Michael began to talk. "I am his guardian. I will stand beside him."

Hospadar looked doubtful. A murmur rose around the room.

Delana's words stilled them. "True, this man has free will, but remember he came to us with goodwill. Let us not forget that. Let us not lose our trust in this man."

"It is the time of testing for all of us." The old man's whispered words were heard by everyone. "We agreed to give the power to man, knowing that the dark forces would be drawn to it. Let us not forget our destiny. The two sides must be reconciled. Is this not your task, Michaal? And is this not possible except by the free covenant of man?"

"All is finished," rang the voice in Ichar's head. "Fino, it is finished." He hated these bright creatures of the sun. He hated the beauty he saw around him. He would destroy their world.

"Ichar." The word entered from beyond himself. Michael was speaking to him. He felt a hand on his shoulder. He let himself be led to the parapet, looked out at the setting sun. "The others have gone, Icharitas. There is just you and I."

Michaal's voice was full of love. "To face this force you have come to Fino. If you can meet it, a new world is possible. If not – " a peace fell between them " – you will kill me, and with that act your bright world will cease to be."

Chapter Eight

"His heart's turned to stone."

"Who?" Pamela felt fear run through her body.

"Doesn't he know we're about more than his copper pennies?"

"Who?" Richard's eyes, cold and glazed, flashed before her. What had he done?

Maia stopped and leaned against the railing. "That blackguard of a baker!" She pointed a finger down the hill toward the village. "The devil take his half-baked scones!"

"What happened?" Pamela took her by the arm, led her inside. "What is it? Sit down."

"Bide alone awhile, Pamela Mary." Maia pulled herself up and went back out, muttering.

Pamela stood, puzzled, for a moment. Then she turned and ran so hard after Maia she almost tripped on the stoop. She grabbed the old woman, dragged her inside, pushed her into a chair. Maia sat and stared straight ahead.

"I'm angry at him." Maia thumped at the table. "I'm angry." She thumped again. "An old woman should be left in peace."

"Stop that." Pamela grabbed for her hands.

Maia rocked forward and back. "There has been an aching in my bones; I told myself it was winter coming on. The ache stiffened my joints; I told myself it was old age creeping upon me." She stopped. "That fool of a baker! He refused me bread." She lifted her arms, but Pamela held her wrists.

"The baker didn't put the ache in your bones," Pamela reminded her. "It wasn't him."

"I'm chilled to my marrow. Put some more peat on the fire, child." Maia got up, walked out again.

"What is it?" Pamela came after her.

She found Maia on the step, her face in her hands. Pamela went to touch her, to try to coax her inside again, but she stepped back. She could see the muscles tense in her shoulders.

"The baker said his yeast had died. He said his bread would not rise."

Pamela sat down beside Maia. "Maia, what is it? It's not the bread. Look at me."

The old woman sat quietly for a moment, then gave a great sigh. "I'm acting wild. Forgive me. It is like a great shadow has fallen across the sun, and I can't see clearly anymore. There is some great evil afoot."

They sat silent for a while, looking out at the storm clouds building over the Atlantic. The wind had come up, cold and raw. Pamela's eyes began to water.

Finally Maia spoke. "Have you heard of the name Lough Derg?"

"Yes, I have heard of it. I didn't know it still existed."

"It has been forgotten. And that is how it was meant to be. For the earth hides her sacred places from the curious." She smiled over at the younger woman. "Lough Derg is such a place, and there is a crying, a desperate calling out for help. I must go to Lough Derg."

"Must you go? Can you not stay here?"

"I wish dearly that I could. Know that I love you more than the daughter I never had. Yet each of us has our task to do."

Pamela felt pride filling the old woman.

"Something is asked of me. In that place it will be made clear. It is a great honor to be able to serve."

"I don't understand."

"A cold wind blows across the earth. With it will come pestilence, earthquakes, even the plague. It has happened before. At Lough Derg there will be given – " Maia paused, then continued almost as if in a trance " – there will be given the words to awaken the earth. She is past being ready. The waters must be divined."

From the tone in Maia's voice, Pamela knew it would be futile to argue.

"I still don't understand, but go if you must."

"Courage. I will be back to greet you in your time." The old woman nodded as if she knew something Pamela didn't.

Pamela could read her so well. "There is more. What is it?"

"You have seen it in all that walk this land: a dullness of eye, a flatness of voice. Lost souls who do the devil's work for him. Pamela, guard the child." The old woman looked her in the face. "I am worried. Something is awry. Can you not hear the wind crying?" She reached across and touched Pamela's hands. "Be fierce as the vixen!"

They sat, feeling the first drops of rain fall from the clouds. The calm of decision was about them.

"I'll miss you," Pamela said quietly. "You've been like a mother to me."

"And you like a daughter. And now you are mother."

"I'm ready."

"Hold the new life precious to you. Wrap it with the light. Hold it firm within your will. The devil is reaching out to claim the unborn as his own."

The next day Maia was gone. Pamela watched her until she disappeared down the road, then up and over a distant hill. Words sprang up in her. "Noble warrior!" Pamela waved, and from the next hilltop the shrunken woman gestured with her stick.

Pamela sat in the doorway, felt the bulk of her belly across her legs, the weight pulling her down. She felt the baby pushing up under her heart. Her breasts felt tender. The old woman was right, she was almost at her time.

She touched her breasts gently. "You've kept me waiting, child." She spoke quietly. "Don't be afraid. I'm keeping watch for you here."

Yesterday's storm looked to be renewing itself. It was getting colder. A wind had come up from the north Atlantic; the shutters began to rattle.

She stood up, looked about her. She was alone again. She needed food and peat. Tomorrow she'd go to the town.

She went inside, closing the door carefully, and started sweeping. She cleaned until night made it impossible. She lit the fire earlier than usual, and beside it turned to her knitting. The clicking of needles sounded loud in the darkness.

Suddenly, the door thumped open. She jumped. "God in heaven! You scared me certain," she exclaimed to the empty room. She closed the door carefully and set the bolt.

The rain pummeled loudly against the slate tiles of the roof. She tried the shutters, but they wouldn't close. Out the darkening window she could see the trees bending as if they would break. *I'm in need of help now*, she thought to herself. She wondered where Jamie O'Ryan was. She prayed that he might come to her.

She lit the candle and watched the shadows form, large and dark around the room. She thought about Maia. The wind howled like a banshee. The sea thrashed against the rock. She shivered.

She tried to reassure the child. "Dear child, do you hear the howling outside? You are safe and snug. Don't be worrying."

Chilling cold rose up from the ocean and flowed in under the door. She threw the last sliver of peat on the fire, but the dampness still probed through the cracks and the windows.

She made up the last of the porridge. She had no more peat to feed the flames. Slowly they flickered and diminished, lower and lower. The shadows grew larger about her. She sat as close to the warmth as she could, faced toward the door. The gale pushed at it, making it creak loudly.

The candle was molten wax in the saucer. She couldn't

move any closer to the fire. The small chapel began to shake. The wind was very strong.

She stared into the darkness, pulled a blanket around her. She crossed her legs. They began to ache. She watched a spider crawl out from a murky shadow and across a strip of light. It didn't belong here. She wanted it to crawl back into the darkness again.

The cold lay across her shoulders; she pulled up her shawl. To comfort herself she tried to sing a lullaby. Her laughter at her own tight singing scared the spider into the shadows. She got up and squashed it, and sat down again, rubbing her hand clean on her apron. "Vermin!" she cried out involuntarily. She watched the fire dim and she kicked up the last of the embers. She tried to remember that day when the sun had burst upon her and filled her with wordless joy. She thought ahead to some future moment when every vein in her being would again flow with liquid light. At this moment the world was still in the embrace of darkness.

"All nights end," she reminded herself.

An animal prowled about outside. She could hear it scratching. She shrank at the thought of it. She watched the candle flicker. "Don't leave me," she called to the little flame. It guttered and went out.

She felt the earth shudder. The floor began to shake.

The sound of her voice frightened her and made her fall silent. She pulled the blanket tighter around her, sat numb in the blackness. She listened to the night noises, held her breath, put her feet flat on the floor. A strength came up through the stone, up through the soles of her feet, the roaring of a thousand rivers pounding up through her body. The earth force was awakening. The quaking stilled.

She could feel the baby kick and she felt a sudden anxiety run through her. For a moment she thought she might burst. She thought of beetles that split in two in birthing.

How much more? she wondered. The nights were still getting longer. She smelled the ashes of the dead fire, dank and acrid. She nodded, half-asleep. Her joints were stiffening.

She jerked herself awake, looked into the darkness. She knew she must not sleep. "Help me," she prayed, trying to imagine even one flicker of light. For a moment, she let herself feel her love for Richard.

This one thing above all others, the thought became part of her: the child must survive. She imagined her child, clear-eyed and unblemished. The ashes from the dead fire swirled up; the cottage smelled of acrid damp. She started at the cold hearth.

"Such a night!" she sighed. "Such a night." She leaned forward to see if there was any dawn light. The window remained a black hole in a black wall. There weren't even any stars.

Slowly, the night began to take shape around her, a dank, cold, cursed shadow. She wondered if perhaps the night felt fear at the coming of the dawn. She imagined it like a scavenger mongrel, sitting up on its haunches. It bared its teeth. It wanted to protect its place. Suddenly she understood night in a new way: it was no different than that part of her shadow, that cold moon of her being.

"Fear not, dog of my shadows. You have your place, and a rightful one."

She was no longer afraid. Just as the day embraced the night, gave it its shape, its form, so the night gave relief from the power of the light. It was but a glimpse into a great mystery, but it was a beginning.

"You need not be so wild." She would call this dark presence closer, touch it with her truth. It whined, bared its teeth and raced away, disappearing within the dark recesses of the far wall. It wasn't ready to be touched.

She knew from this moment evil's own fear – its fear of being devoured and taken into the light. She saw its fear of being no more, of being annihilated by the light.

She felt almost a gentleness toward it, a compassion. It would only harm her if she tried to deny it its rightful place. Her fear lessened.

She stood, feet apart by the cold hearth, felt the waters of the earth pulsing up through her feet, felt the power of life full within her. In the thin growing light, she could see the stone walls of the chapel. The winds had died away. Exhausted, she leaned against the hearth.

She woke in the cold of early morning. Opening her eyes, she stretched, shook herself free of the cold and sat up. The walls were bright now. She sensed in herself a curious lightness. She needed to go into Enniscrone.

The sun was only a dull brightness low in the sky. Everything was washed clean by the storm. She walked the distance to town, whistling quietly to herself.

She tried the door of the wool shop. Locked. Shades were

pulled down in the other shops. Where had everyone gone? She ran down a lane, hurried along a narrow street of stone houses. There was not a soul in sight anywhere.

A dog ran up to her. She rubbed his ears and talked to him. "Not barking today are you, fine friendly dog? Tell me, where have they all gotten to?"

A heavy clanging of bells came to her ears. She laughed. "Sunday. It must be Sunday." She gave the dog a pat, thanked it and lifted the shawl over her head. She walked toward the sound of the bells.

Pamela stood at the back of the small chapel, just inside the door. The celebrant at the foot of the altar stood with his back to the congregation. He began his *Confiteo Deo*. "I confess to Almighty God that I have sinned...through my fault, through my fault..."

She watched as he lifted his head up to the crucified form of the Christ and beat his chest. "Through my most grievous fault." His voice was thick with guilt.

She watched him limp up the altar steps to begin the sacrifice of the mass. He kissed the altar stone and turned to the congregation. "The Lord be with you."

Unable to help herself, she gasped. Her hand moved instinctively to her own face. His eyes looked directly at her.

"And with you," she joined in the response. The side of his face was red with an enormous birthmark.

The young priest turned back to the altar.

What must it be like? she wondered. *All the days of his life! In each person he met, the reflection in the eyes. He must wait for it, look for it, demand it. To bear that mark.*

This was what had been carried forward – the mark of Cain upon the race: asking forgiveness, begging, carrying the guilt, crucifying, sacrificing. All to no avail.

She watched as the mass progressed. The sacrifice of the body and blood of Christ repeated endlessly, each time in the hope that someday he would come and take away this mark of sin. The old forms were changing – that she knew.

She moved forward to the altar rail to take communion. She watched the priest as he put the unleavened wafer on the tongue of each communicant. Pamela stepped closer to the rail. The young priest stood in front of her, wondering, she supposed, why she was not on her knees.

She looked into his face, waiting for an invitation, a gesture, a simple asking. He looked at her; the truth was in his eyes. "Help me, hold me," they said.

She stepped forward, took his face in her hands and kissed the birthmark.

The mark of Cain was gone forever.

Chapter Nine

Ichar dawdled on his way to the Phoenix; he continued to ponder last night's dream. He had been handed a great torch. But it had burned his hand and he had thrown it to the ground. Then an old woman appeared and picked it up, and made him take it back, only it wasn't him anymore; he was now someone else looking on. He watched, horrified, as this other self put the torch to the house he was living in. Furious, he had leaped on this other part of himself. The two of them had crashed to the ground, smashing at one another. He'd awakened dripping with sweat, his head aching.

He felt a little clearer now; there was a lull on the battleground inside himself. He was in a world of light and warmth, yet inside there lived a creature of darkness and spite. If only he could gain control over this creature, whatever it was. When it spoke up inside him, he was powerless. He prayed that he might be given the strength to control himself.

He had been sick all morning with vomiting and diarrhea. At least, for these few minutes, he felt more or less himself. It was such a relief. Yet he knew the creature was growing stronger in him, threatening to overcome him completely. He stopped at the stairwell leading up to the Phoenix. Whatever it was, it had entered him. His world seemed to hang in the balance. He started up the stairs.

"Good morning, Ichar." Delana met him on the patio. She smiled, radiant with the morning sun. "You look exhausted." She took his arm. "Come." She led him across the patio.

He could smell gardenias about her, feel softness flow through her hand to comfort him. The voice was beginning again. He turned his eyes away from her. Perhaps it was true – that he didn't deserve such love. It was hard not to believe the voice. Unknowingly, he was falling into its grip.

He watched her study his face. What was she thinking? Even if she poured herself out, poured out her love for him, he knew it would not be enough. Surely she must know that.

She walked with him up the spiral stairs. "Michaal will meet us in the upper chamber. After the meeting last evening, I thought it might be better for the three of us to talk together."

Ichar nodded. "I never thought it would be this way. I can't seem to help myself."

"We cannot explain it, either. Suddenly you changed. What was it around the vessel that changed you so?"

Ichar shook his head. He could no longer recall.

"Remember we are here with you. All our strength is yours."

Ichar pondered the situation. They understood light,

these people of Fino. If they were to help him, they would also have to learn to understand darkness.

They entered the upper chamber. Delana watched him intently. He gazed at an onyx sculpture of dolphins, then was struck by the marble figure near the balustrade. He wondered again what Delana was thinking.

She moved over to the figure, put her hand on its torn face, gazed back at him. "Ichar."

"It's horrible," he muttered. "It looks like a cripple – one leg missing, his arms torn away." He was surprised at the intensity of his reaction. "Even the face is shattered." His voice sounded strange and thick.

"It was destroyed in the Maelstrom," said Delana. She caressed the statue gently. "I have always had such a fondness for it. I don't know why." She continued to move her hands over it slowly. "I care for it very much. Even now it fills the room with its grandeur. It's the fountainhead from the square. It's still beautiful, isn't it?"

Ichar stopped, amazed. So here was the centerpiece! It had been here all this time. "What happened?"

"It is just as we found it, down beside the fountain. It was broken in the Maelstrom." She sat down, beckoned for Ichar to join her. "Michaal will be here soon. He promised to bring us breakfast."

Ichar felt himself nod. He looked at his hands, watched as his thumb pushed itself into the palm of his other hand.

"It could be rebuilt," he suggested. "New limbs could be carved out of wood and fixed to the stone."

Yes, I could rebuild it, he thought to himself. He knew enough to make the fountain whole. He saw water flowing up again through the centerpiece.

Looking up, he wondered how long he had been lost in thought. Michaal stood before him, holding out a glass goblet.

"Good morning. It's good to see you. I've made you a warm drink."

"Thank you." Ichar took the goblet, noting the crystal inlays.

"It will help," Michaal said, and sat down beside him.

Ichar moved away, holding his drink untasted. Michaal was always the same, young and radiant like a column of light. But why, he reasoned, should Michaal have so much, he so little? Why did he, Ichar, have to be the cripple? One day, he promised, he would balance the scales. It was not fair. Both of them should have nothing.

He tasted the yellow drink, rich on his tongue. His thoughts returned to the marble figure. They could have simply dumped it on the trash heap. But they had rescued it.

"They should have smashed it to dust." Inside him the voice rose in volume.

He shook his head at the thought. He pondered the sculpture, its face torn, its leg ripped off. He got up and moved toward the statue. He wanted to explain his ideas to Delana and Michaal.

"I could make the arms of oak." He gestured so his friends could see. "They would be strong then."

"What are they holding?" Delana asked.

As he studied the sculpture, the face became whole in his mind. The eyes came to life, blue, clear and happy. A beautiful smile appeared on the mouth. He closed his eyes. It was possible. He could do it. He would rebuild the image he saw before him. It would be strong, with loving arms.

"What is he holding?" Delana was waiting for an answer.

He saw it as it had been, as it could be again. The statue stood whole, unflawed, resurrected from the ruins.

"A child!" The words tumbled from his mouth. "A child." He saw himself holding a child in his arms. A man, madonnalike, holding a newborn child.

"Michaal!" Delana stood as if struck. "This man is indeed the childbearer." She moved a step forward, then paused as she watched his mood change.

It was not yet so and never would be. He knew he would let her down. He always failed her. He felt like he was teetering on some brink. The voice inside was hungry. "Get to the child quickly. Keep it from being born. The child will destroy us." The voice pounded in his head.

"But the child is so beautiful, so young and so helpless." When he spoke, his own voice sounded thin, powerless. Then he felt his body being possessed by a dark, hot rage. He shouted out, "The child is ugly, ugly as sin."

He could feel Michaal grabbing for his shoulders.

"Look at me. You're here among those who love you."

Ichar wanted to avoid those eyes that held him firm and caring, but for some reason he dared a glance. He caught his breath. For an instant he saw Michaal's infinite love. It was too much. He did not deserve such love.

He knew the rot in his being; knew he would destroy this love. He had betrayed this man before. He deserved only damnation. He felt himself slumping down onto the floor. From somewhere he could hear his own words: "It is my fault, my fault, my grievous fault." His guilt swallowed him whole.

"Get him to the couch."

Delana must have helped Michaal because he seemed to feel many hands holding him. A long way off, he could hear Michaal speaking.

"He did let us in. He did see us, if only for a moment. That might make some difference."

"You must keep close to him. Do not let him slip away." Delana sounded urgent. "Talk to him."

"Ichar, we walked together, ran through the grasslands, swam in the sea, bathed in the sunlight."

Ichar reached up with his hand.

"I am here, Ichar."

"I am tired and old. Carry me on your back."

"You are strong; rest awhile."

"No, no. I am weak. You must carry me." He sucked at Michaal's strength.

"You have the strength of a warrior." Michaal's hand was firm.

"Carry me, Michaal, I cannot walk."

His other hand was taken by the smaller palms of Delana. He felt terribly tired. "Fight, Ichar," she urged.

"Michaal, I need you. Forget her." He jerked his hand

away from Delana's. "We two together – quick, to the vessel!"

"Be strong, Ichar, I have not left you."

"The vessel, quick, to the other side. Leave her. The woman is cursed. It is you I want."

"Your only hope, Ichar, is in both of us."

"We together – come away. We can create our own world."

"We are here, Ichar. The three of us. We will win through."

"I will destroy this bright world. This day you'll be with me in hell."

"Michaal, don't. He would drag you into himself."

Ichar could feel Delana's hand on his forehead. He could smell the stench of his fear. "Don't touch me!" He screamed until she took her hand away from his face. "Get away, whore!"

"The statue, Ichar." Her voice was firm. "What part is missing? Tell me about the part that was lost."

Ichar felt himself become rigid.

"The child, Ichar." She was whispering now. "Are you afraid to hold it? Afraid you will destroy it? Is that what hounds you? You won't destroy the child. Trust yourself."

"I came that – that the child would live." He was stammering. He felt so weak. His stomach ached. The voice was stronger than his will. He could hear it speaking more and more loudly. "You want to leave me outside in the darkness forever. But I've fooled you all. I've wormed my way into your bright world and now I have you. And soon I will have the child."

"No! You came to protect the child, Ichar. You can do it!" Delana urged.

"My kind is beyond redemption."

"Ichar, this is the test. Do not believe this."

"I am the curse of man." He could feel his nails digging into his thighs. "Man always kills that which he loves."

"There is another way." The woman's voice entered the darkness.

"No. Your womb is empty as the void. In you, the new life will be stillborn." An animal was howling. He saw the earth, cold and void, a sterile womb in a dead universe. He laughed wildly. "Now I have you!" Black flames rose up around him. He clawed at the empty air.

Their hands held him firmly. He lay, his eyes closed, as they protected him from himself, cleaned his body, wrapped him in fresh linen.

"Michaal, my strength is all but gone. He is all but lost to us."

"I will destroy the Medieglot," he declared.

"Michaal." Her voice was strained, thin. "We need help. We must call on the others."

Chapter Ten

About noon Pamela heard a knocking at the door. She opened it. There he stood, his peaked hat in his hand, a huge package under his arm.

"Jamie O'Ryan!"

He smiled; a soft radiance flowed from him. "I had a thought you might be needing some repairs done."

She took his hand and pulled him in. "Sit yourself down."

He looked about him. "A cozy place you have here, Pamela."

"Indeed, Jamie. It's here I mean to have my child."

"Still it does need a little fixing."

"There is a draft under the door and the shutters won't close."

Jamie nodded.

She laughed at his mock seriousness. "How do you like me now, fat and barrel-shaped as I am?" She gave him a full profile and then danced about for him. "Oh, Jamie, it's good to see you!" She hugged him. It felt good to hold him close. She held him gently. Then she released him.

"I've thought of you often, Pamela." He picked up the package, set it on the table, started to pull apart the heavy brown paper. "I wanted my gift to be the crib." He stood back.

She rocked it forward and back, ran her hand along the oiled wood. It was beautiful. She looked at the mother-of-pearl carefully inlaid in the dark wood. "Exquisite," she whispered. "It's truly grand, Jamie, grand. You couldn't have brought me a better gift."

He was such a gentle man, Pamela reflected, looking over at him. He had been at her side ever since she could remember, like an older brother, the guardian, O'Ryan.

"I'll put the tea on."

"There's no hurry." He sat down, looked at her.

She felt the warmth of her blush. She set out the cups and saucers.

"There were many stories told after you ran off. For a while, the people of Kinvarra thought you'd thrown yourself into the sea."

"I wandered up the coast starving myself half to death."

"Gradually word got back of a witch living alone in a hill shack near Enniscrone. I thought it might be you."

"I was quite beside myself for weeks with no food, only the wind and the banshees to haunt me."

"Then word returned of a saintly woman living in a stone chapel overlooking the sea. It had to be you."

She straightened her apron and laughed. "If only they knew!" She got up and made the tea. She watched it steep;

for some reason, thoughts of her father came to mind. She waited until Jamie had finished his tea. Then she turned to him with the question that had been haunting her. "Why did he leave me?"

Jamie looked confused.

"My father, I mean. Why did he leave me?"

Jamie shifted in his chair and answered in a quiet voice, "He was recalled to Centrex. He had to go."

"No, no. Jamie, more than that. You know...."

He gave her a long assessing look. Then he nodded slightly to himself. "Then think about this. Would you have got to Centrex if he had stayed?"

She sat silent, pulled at her skirt. "But he left me, Jamie! Why? It must have been something I did."

"No, Pamela. It wasn't you." He stopped, waited a moment. "Pamela, he knew you would be hurt. He himself was hurt. But how could he tell you that it was necessary, that he loved you, that in the end..." He slipped his hand into his jacket pocket.

"All my life I thought it was something I had done, Jamie." There were tears in her eyes; she was surprised at herself.

He reached out and held her hand the way he had when she had been a little girl he took to market. When she opened her hand, she found in it a pearl, a soft blue-gray pearl pulsing warm and translucent in her palm.

"For me?"

He nodded. "Yes, your father gave it to me before you were

born. He knew that a time would come when you would need to know about him. It is his birth gift to you."

Pamela stroked and rolled the pearl in her hands.

"He wanted me to give it to you with these words: 'My child, no words or deeds can carry through time my love for you. Yet may this pearl be as a token, and a sign of a greater gift to come.'"

She held the exquisite sea gem glowing in her hand, and watched as her tears fell onto it. She remembered that night in the stairwell. She looked down at the pearl: something so beautiful from a small speck of dirt. "Just like him," she cried aloud. "Just like him."

Jamie cleared away the cups and saucers, started the fire in the hearth.

Pamela came over, sat beside him and stared into the fire, her head propped in her hands.

"Jamie?"

"Yes."

"What about my mother, then?"

"I visit Alice often..."

"No, no, Jamie. The truth."

"Pamela, Alice doesn't talk as much as she did before your last visit. In fact, she usually just sits quietly and stares out in front of her, as if she is traveling in some far place at the back of her mind. She is a remarkable woman, Pamela. I don't think you realize it, but she kept you alive – your spirit, I mean."

Pamela nodded.

"She pushed at you, never let you fall back into self-pity or hopelessness. By herself alone, she did it. Do you know what that means?"

For a while, Pamela sat. Into her mind came a memory of her first day of school. Her mother was walking beside her. She remembered how frightened she'd been of the older children, how scared she'd been of leaving her mother, how she'd been feeling so sorry for herself. For some reason, her mother's words that day had remained in her mind. "If you were a boy now, I wouldn't have to be walking you to school, with you whimpering like a puppy dog."

All the fear and self-pity had burned off in a split second of raw anger. She remembered how she'd pulled her hand away, run off to the school ground. She had never looked back. It had been that fiery anger that had taken her through school with honors, taken her to Dublin and on to Centrex. She understood in a flash what her mother had done for her.

"That anger – she fostered that." Pamela looked up. "Jamie, I understand better now."

In the days that followed, the chapel was repaired. The hearth was well stoked for night, and the fear that stalked the lonely held at bay. And so the two friends spent their time working and chatting, waiting for the great event.

One day, a day of sunlight and cloud shadows, she heard Jamie round the corner of the chapel, talking to someone.

Pamela dropped the laundry she had been pinning up and

ran around to the front. "Maia!" Pamela ran into her arms. She felt love flowing from the old woman. "It's so good to see you." She wiped away the tears. "I've missed you."

Maia's eyes twinkled. "You're looking radiant, you are, Pamela. Radiant as a pea pod about to pop. Not for one moment were you out of my heart." The two stood, floating on the pleasure between them.

Pamela linked her arm with Maia's, then reached over and took Jamie's hand. "Maia, meet my friend, Jamie O'Ryan. He came up from Galway to help with the chores. It's been a boon having him here."

Her two friends surveyed each other.

"And who, O'Ryan, are you?" Maia asked.

"I spend my days on the sea, putting my nets deep into the Atlantic, making my livelihood in an honest way. I am a fisherman."

Pamela cut in. "Maia, Maia, Jamie is the one I've spoken so much about. From the time I was small, he was always across the street. He has grown up with me."

But Jamie was speaking again. "And who in the great heavens are you?"

"I walk the land finding water for those who want it. I am a dowser."

"I have heard of you often."

Maia nodded. Then she looked toward Pamela. "Come, join with us, Pamela."

Pamela stepped forward. The old woman moved her hands as if weaving a circle around the three of them. Pamela could feel the hair at the nape of her neck stand on end. Then, as if a spell had been cast, Maia relaxed.

"Fisherman, we'll be needing a forked branch." She turned to Pamela. "My dear, did I hear you tell of a hazel tree in the ravine?"

"Yes, it's at the end of the line of oak trees."

"Good. Hazel is what we'll need. But let me catch my breath. Is there some bread and cheese? I feel famished."

Maia went on talking as Jamie fetched food, but she declined to enter the chapel. She seated herself on the front step.

Pamela could not hold back her questions any longer. "But Maia, Maia – what about Lough Derg?"

The old woman smiled. "Ah. I'll tell you about Lough Derg. The rock beds of Lough Derg speak of an earth change undreamed of by our forefathers. Fisherman, know you that underfoot, the earth is ready to draw down the very stars in heaven?"

"Aye. In the Atlantic, the tides swell to new heights, as if they would reach to touch the sky."

Jamie set out the food and they ate in silence. After Pamela had cleared the table, Maia started to talk again. "We must all do our part." She looked at Jamie. "Fisherman, will you fetch the hazel fork now?"

"I will indeed." Picking up the hatchet by the stoop, Jamie headed off along the row of oaks.

"Come and sit down beside me, Pammie." The old woman talked in a whisper. "When I walked the stones of

Lough Derg, I felt a new life beginning to stir in the earth's core. There was a longing within the stone itself to be called upward into life. A force is moving. Woman's voice is needed to call it forth. Your word will flesh the union of what will be."

"But of man?"

"I see a despair so deep within man that he could destroy everything. He has become one with the darkness. But if we all do our part..."

Pamela sat staring blankly at the wall behind the old woman. "Last night, I dreamed that Richard had fallen into a bottomless pit. Yet as he fell, I could see his eyes looking to me. For a brief moment he saw me. I know he did! Then he fell away into darkness. But the despair had gone from his eyes."

"Then maybe all is not lost. Even Lucifer himself might yet be saved." The old woman chuckled to herself at the possibility. "Come, Pamela. We have work to do. If the man wins through, all must be made ready.

"Where is that Jamie-person anyway?" Maia laughed again.

"He's coming up the walk now."

"It is about time, isn't it?"

Jamie came up with a forked piece of hazel. Quickly he shaped it into a dowsing wand, passed it across to Maia. She felt its heft and its spring. The wood seemed to come alive in her hands. It quivered and plunged with such energy that Maia had to grip hard to keep hold of it. "Never have I divined such power. Pamela, you have chosen your birthing place well. Now let us draw up this force." She walked a little toward the oak trees. Jamie and Pamela followed.

The old woman looked at the ground and spoke quietly. "What we are about is the quickening of the earth. The earth is stirring, awakening. The force of this can erupt in earthquake or storm, or it can be drawn upward into consciousness. Just remember, we are not alone. If this force can be contained and channeled, it will bring upon us a new dawning."

"Aye. As did the Fisherman of Nazareth, long years ago."

"Anything is possible. Now, let us move out from this chapel. The earth currents spin out from a point of power like the spiral of a seashell. The hazel fork will guide us. But first we must ready ourselves."

The old woman blessed Jamie, then Pamela, with an ancient sign. "Now, Pamela, place your hands over me."

Pamela made the sign as she had seen Maia do.

"Now," she continued. "Repeat after me these words: We join ourselves with that being who is earth. One are we with the dark soil. One are we with her waters. One are we with her source."

Slowly they moved in procession out from the chapel; earth woman in the lead drawn forward by the quivering hazel fork, Pamela in the center, fisherman behind, staff in hand. With each widening gyre out from the chapel center, the air became heavier. The hazel wand took on life, at times almost wrenching itself out of the old woman's hands.

171

Pamela could feel the earth currents rising up through her. She leaned her head back and felt the sun's warmth on her face.

From behind her came the words of fisherman: "From the ruins of the Phoenix will come the warrior. A warrior fierce enough to enter the darkness; a warrior without weapon save his own goodwill. By daring the portals, he will close them. Redeem the Iscariot, return with the one who was lost."

Pamela heard herself say "Amen" after his words. Outward they continued in their spiral, circling the chapel again and again. Earth woman's body quivered now as much as the hazel fork she held. Her speech was thick with an ancient chant, beyond word or meaning. Gradually, the chant began to make sense to Pamela, as though the old woman had started speaking a language she knew.

"From the point of light we call the sun, let light stream down into this source we call the earth." Pamela felt the sunlight strike her head, pass down through her body. She felt herself glowing, translucent.

"From the source of life, deep within the dark of earth, let the waters rise up to join with the light." Pamela felt a cool flow, almost like water, rise up through her. A current rose up through the soles of her feet, passed through her, left through the crown of her head and rose up into the heavens. Then it dropped down around her like an invisible fountain, back onto the earth.

She breathed deeply and spoke: "From a place in time beyond day and night, from a point of love within earth and sky, come forth a healing no man has yet ordained." The child in her womb stirred.

Onward the procession moved, out into wider and wider circles. With each step the power grew about them. Like ancient sorcerers, the three invoked the forces of earth and sky. But still something seemed unspoken. The new life in her womb waited, but for what? What did she need to do?

Earth woman stumbled. Fisherman stopped to help her to her feet. Pamela walked on alone. For an instant she had a vision of what was asked of her. The dark child reached out to her.

Chapter Eleven

Michaal sat opposite Delana on the patio of the Phoenix. Evening had given them some relief from the struggle of the day. Ichar lay asleep in the upper chamber, a shell of what he had been.

Gradually, one by one, the patio filled with the workers of the Medieglot. Michaal felt restored by the familiar presences as they gathered about him. All of them had been touched by the edge of that force he had long since banished from this world; they assembled tonight in their concern. Together, they must find another way.

Michaal waited until the gathering was complete. Around him, he sensed the Seraphim and Powers. Sensed, too, the presence of the masters who had, at one time or another, walked the earth in human guise. All of these beings had been rejected from the human plane. Like Michaal's, their power was limited to containment. All they could do was reject, and therefore limit, the dark force within matter. They could do no more. Yet they still hoped. It was now up to those who still walked that world. Who could choose, who could change everything in the blinking of an eye.

They stood together, powerful but helpless. The man, Icharitas, had given them new hope, for his goodwill had allowed them to make contact. But now he, too, was on the verge of being lost.

Michaal opened his mind to his cohorts. "Icharitas has fallen back. At present he is containing the darkness, but for how much longer, I do not know. The whole sphere of the Medieglot is at risk."

Michaal reflected on the many times man had attempted to face the curse that had tormented his race and the many times he had fallen back.

"It's not a curse – remember that. It's the root of man's power and it will be his glory." The thought arose from the Supreme Logos itself. Michaal found this idea hard to grasp. He knew little of darkness; all he knew was that man believed he had to protect it with his guilt. He could see mankind, shuffling along, wearing guilt like a mantle, a badge of bondage.

"This is what saps man's strength – his guilt. This is what humanity must somehow lift from itself." The message came again from the Supreme Logos.

Delana's thought sparkled. "Yes! Guilt is the shield mankind thinks he must use, and all the while behind it, the voice has created a place that is safe for itself." Poor creatures. She felt pity, compassion. She understood Ichar's weakness now; if he could forgive himself his past, lift from himself that terrible guilt, the future might be changed.

"This, then, is the task before you – to help them," the Supreme Logos continued. "You have come forward, all of you, to serve this race. Through your involvement, humankind, this world, yourselves will all evolve."

"But they have chosen to bury themselves in instinct, in matter. It is we who are denied access." Raheem's thought echoed with sadness.

"But we need to be honest about the task." The thought arose from a small, fragile being.

Michaal waited.

The thought unfolded in meaning. "We are not, I deem, utterly beyond fear ourselves. It is an enormous risk to trust them. We know fear just in taking this risk. And if we are afraid, what then of them? They are the frailest of all spirits. They live in a fear we cannot begin to imagine."

Delana's thought brightened. "What for them is fear, is in fact a way of knowing. They were born open to darkness so they could learn the truth at its heart. I would risk all I have to help."

"But so much horror, waste. Could you face that?" Michael asked.

"Yes."

"Could you love my dark child?" The question, almost a plea coming from the heart of the Supreme Logos, stunned them all. The heavens fell hushed. All awaited her word.

Delana looked within. She knew what was being asked – for her to embrace the pain, the hurt, the horror of all that was human.

They waited.

"Yes, I would love your child."

A gratitude simple and pure filled the ether. Michaal stood in awe of her courage, watched as she thinned and departed into that sphere of earth travail.

Slowly the thought of the Supreme Logos formed within him. "Michaal, can you see your way clear to what you must do?"

Michaal hesitated uncertain.

The Supreme Logos continued, "Are you not his guardian? Did you not take final charge of him? You did all you could, but is there not something you omitted to do?"

Michaal answered slowly, "It is true I am his guardian. I did shape the world of Fino around him that he might be made ready. I did prepare the vessel." He sensed the stillness in the listening spirits.

Into the silence came the question. "But did you tell him he would be the helmsman? Does he know that we trust him? That, despite all, he is to steer the vessel? That it was made for him?"

"I told him only that the vessel was made to my specifications."

"Now we know how the plague entered Fino."

Michael trembled, naked before the truth. "It was hard to believe he was ready to take the helm."

Sequitus's thought shone with clarity. "So it is we who must demonstrate the first trust – we who have the power."

"Michaal, Countenance of the Sun." The Supreme Logos spoke again. "You prepared the vessel. Within it, your light would enter man's plane. You would front Centrex with a brilliance beyond their wildest imaginings. You would win them from darkness by the force of your light. Michaal, Light Bearer, know that the knowledge of darkness is my gift to man. As my light is to you.

"Know also that man's destiny is your destiny. This you must never forget." The Logos continued, "Your task is to trust. The vessel will be weak, fragile, human. But it is to him you must pledge your strength. Man at this moment is the helmsman of evolution. That is why he was given into your special keeping.

"Michaal, Sword of Light. You who have never known weakness, never experienced darkness, known only light, truth, love, power. Will you put aside your sword? Will you endow this man with your power? Enter his travail? Trust his will?"

Michaal looked upon Ichar, saw the long journey of this soul he had grown to love, knew this man's pain and struggle.

"The reward is great beyond comprehension…the end of the Great Enmity."

The heavens fell hushed. Time stopped. All of creation awaited his response.

A flash of radiant light burst across the firmament, and with this fiat Michaal began to sense human frailty. A taste of doubt entered his mind. He looked toward where Delana had been. Suddenly he knew that she had taken the same step, before him. They would go forward together.

He became aware of feelings he had never before felt or

understood: the thickness of human love, the anguish of the human heart, the fear that all could be lost in the blinking of an eye.

He felt himself transported to the upper chamber. His strength filled Icharitas, his light flowed into his veins. He reached out to this man's will for good, and gave himself in final trust into his keeping.

Chapter Twelve

Icharitas lay, afraid to open his eyes, afraid he had done the deed, afraid that he had destroyed all that was dear to him. He fell back into the relief of sleep, aware, somehow, that a decision had been reached that would save his life. He woke again to a great surge through his blood, as though a blinding flash had burst across the sky from horizon to horizon. About him he sensed a great massing of spirits, as if he was being held suspended in some cosmic womb. He lay with his eyes closed. There had been a time when he had refused such thoughts, when he had banished such presences from his mind.

There it was again. "Ichar, we are here." He opened his eyes and saw them about him the joyful smiling faces – Raheem, David, Hospadar – all of them.

"Ic." David was holding his hand.

"I'm here, too." Raheem straightened his hair.

He was naked before them: all he was, was not, lay revealed. They groomed him, combed him.

"I feel no shame." He was amazed at himself.

"There is no shame."

"No guilt?"

"None!" they sang to him. "All is as it should be."

Guilt fell from his shoulders. He lay back; the gardenias' perfume seemed to crown his heart. Once again he could walk with them; together they would renew the earth. He had not betrayed them. They lived. The joy of that truth let him hope again. A strength he had never known before filled him.

Richard, with his eyes closed, listened to the murmuring around him.

"We must fade from his vision. We no longer need to be seen. It is now between him and his voice." The quiet tones drew back. "Give him his dignity. He will fight in his own way."

Slowly, as if in a dream, vision came. He could see the way clear before him. He knew how he would begin. He stood up from the couch, stretched as a man would awakening from a long sleep and walked across the upper room to the ancient centerpiece.

He examined the mutilated torso in detail. It was about his own height. The right leg was missing below the knee, the left arm broken off just below the shoulder, right hand snapped off, the face smashed – probably where it had toppled onto the cobblestones. The rest was well-weathered – pocked with age, but still intact.

He heaved the figure onto his shoulders, carried it across the patio and down the narrow steps cut through the rock, out into the square. He placed it down next to the fountain.

He smiled as he remembered the old man working on the winged figure. He knew now how he would maintain his purpose. Even when choked by the voice, he knew his hands would be able to hold him true to his intent. He began to search for the things he would need.

"He does not see us." Raheem was puzzled.

"He has entered a plane sacrosanct unto himself, a plane sacred to his race. It is there he will shape the new form; there he will transmute light and darkness into form. Let us be as witness."

Richard looked up. He thought he'd heard voices, but the square remained empty. Only the fountain trickled quietly near him. He breathed deeply and focused his thought on the task before him. He would need a chisel. He headed up to the workshop, took a sheath of chisels, picked up a whetstone and went to the wood bin. He searched until he found what he needed – several pieces of oak with a close grain, and one piece of black walnut.

He had to make several trips before he assembled all the necessary tools. He spent some time considering the wood he would use for the leg. It didn't have to be a large piece, but it had to be able to hold the weight of the marble. It also had to be burred in such a way that he could shape heel and foot without the grain splitting.

Finally, he set to work. His hands moved slowly and clumsily, getting in the way of his eagerness. Yet he worked with the wood carefully. He would restore to this figure a beauty it had never before known. Despite his eagerness the raw matter, akin to his nature, resisted the blade. Firmly holding the wood, he chiseled away at it, slowly and patiently.

His vision was locked to his will. The past would be healed, the future freed. He gave shape to this purpose, saw in his mind how the myriad splinters of wood that fell about him were like seeds. He whistled to himself, happy with his work.

Suddenly the voice rose in his head. "Don't let them out!" The voice bit and chipped at him. "Don't let them out. It will be to your undoing!"

"They are already out."

"Your will is rotten!" the voice condemned. "You are the source of the Maelstrom."

"They are the seed of the new," he challenged.

"Delusion!" the voice hissed.

He focused his attention on the slow shaping of the wood before him.

"You hold new life." He thought he could hear Pamela speaking to him; she sounded tender, sure.

"I hold new life," he repeated stubbornly, keeping his attention on the wood. He believed her. For the moment he was safe.

The voice diminished to mumbles, sank away inside him. He would have to be wary. It, too, wanted to be free, he realized. It, too, had its place, and for the first time, he sensed a new possibility.

He exulted in his newfound strength. The chisel moved carefully into the wood; a large chip fell to the ground.

Already the shape of the leg was emerging. He picked up the mallet, began on the foot. The air was perfumed with fresh-cut oak. The work was going well; he felt proud of himself. For just a moment he relaxed his intent and he was, again, instantly possessed.

"You know you're lost, Richard." The voice sobbed, plaintive, seductive. He couldn't help but listen. "You are lost in time, far from home…far from home…far from home…."

He nodded drowsily.

"You can't remember who you are. You have forgotten what you're here for. You have forgotten why you came." Forgotten…forgotten…

His will weakened. He saw himself warming his hands beside a fire. He knew it was important to wake, but couldn't remember why. The fire felt warm and he was sleepy. He smelled the flesh of a corpse. He lifted his head and looked into the fire. But it wasn't a fire – it was the rotting corpse of a goat, the rotting remains of a scapegoat, and he was warming his hands upon its heat. He stood up, sick to his stomach.

He would wander forever. The dust from the road coated his flesh; he had grown hoary with frost. Clay stiffened his bones. It had been silly to try. Nothing mattered anymore. Forward he went, open-eyed, into limbo; a stone of flesh on the roadside, a soul lost in the ancient labyrinth of the mind. He tasted the putrid sweetness of his self-pity. He had tried; surely that was enough.

Gradually, he became aware of a burning that pierced his hand. The pain of his own flesh cut through to him.

He came to with a start. There was blood on his hand; his chisel was on the ground. A jagged cut gaped across his palm and oozed blood. He soaked his hand in the clear, cool water that was rising in the fountain, bandaged it with a piece of fabric he tore from his shirt, returned to his work. His will would be done. He tended to his appointed task.

He no longer chased through the twists and turns of the labyrinth, but set to work tearing it down, chip by chip. Guilt, sin, duty, shame. He imagined the rebirth of his world. He would walk the wasteland, water the dry soil. One day his kind would husband the land with love. He imagined the garden he would call forth for his offspring, a green place where sunlight would play amidst the shadows.

Late each night – for sleep was no longer safe – he chiseled and planed, cut and carved. The task was before him: to join stone and wood, death and life, past and future, spirit and matter into wholeness. And as he trusted, the way opened before him.

For days and nights without end, he worked on. He finished the arms, fastened them in place , stood the statue upright. It looked larger than life, a warrior of some ancient clan. It waited by the fountain with neither shield nor sword. The water was welling up, spreading across the square. His sense of accomplishment was so great that he was unaware of the pulsing flow of fresh water.

Now for the child. He searched about for the piece of black walnut. This would have to be shaped solely with a knife. He sat on the rim of the fountain and began to work. He watched the wood shape itself into the form of an infant. Because he was whistling, he did not hear the shrill edge of the voice as it stole into his mind.

Slowly, the world changed about him. He was standing beside Michaal, on the vessel under the clear night sky. Michaal was at the helm. The moon hung low, a dull sickle. Richard watched as Ichar came up behind Michaal, called softly to him.

Michaal turned and Ichar took him in a cold embrace. He watched over Michaal's shoulder as his own hand raised the knife and plunged it into Michaal's back. Michaal looked into his eyes with a gaze of such penetrating betrayal. Ichar pulled the bloody blade out of his back. The bow of the boat caught a wave and careened off, out of control. Ichar found himself pushed up against the cockpit, the dying body of Michaal convulsed against him, the blood, wet and warm. The boat tightened its mad circling and Richard saw only sea meeting sky in a spinning chaos of stars and waves and madness. He was free at last. Free...

He had freed himself of his great love. He had spilled his own blood. But the act had given him no relief, not even emptiness – just the agony that goes beyond horror, the agony of the betrayer.

The ship spun past him, the sea and sky dizzying in their whirlpool vortex. He spun in the Maelstrom, down into the pit, down into the darkness. He was Judas the Betrayer, beyond redemption. He saw in the cold brilliance of that black light, himself – forever doomed. At every birth, he would stand, an urchin on the left side, embracing the new child. He would wait until they, too, renounced the light and paid homage to the cold chill of dead flesh.

He was evil, murderer of life, forever and ever, world without end. He stood mute, frozen in hell. But through his veins, he could feel another reality, a thin hope that flickered like the stars far above. He found himself waiting, listening, hoping. He recognized the rushing sound of water welling up. It seemed to have a voice of its own. "I'm here," he seemed to hear. "I'm here within you."

He felt the splash of water upon his face. Richard pushed the dark vision of what might have been from himself, opened his eyes to the spraying rush of water up from the plinth. He saw the knife in his hand, saw the black walnut. The child was taking shape. Soon it would be ready to be placed within the arms of the fountain piece he would place on the plinth.

His hands had helped him win through. He exulted in his strength and allowed himself to feel something he never had before: joy in knowing his race could one day be made whole. Cleansed by this truth, he began to sense how it could be done.

Like a dream upon waking, the dark vision remained with him – an open doorway into the pit. Suddenly Richard knew what was being asked of him. The voice lurked in the shadows, waiting for a moment of weakness. His soul shone like a column of light. "Come," he called out to the voice. "Come forward. I would see you as you are." The blackness skulked, a serpent in the shadows. Richard put down his chisel, stood steadily on the threshold into night.

"I have come for you!" Richard leaped forward. He charged down, driven by a ferocious urge to clash with the arch foe. Astride the light, he sped into the pit, raced down through his being – deep in chase, hot in pursuit. Aflame with the pure white rage of love, Richard charged into the center of the Maelstrom.

Out of the blackness, buzzing, stinging creatures came at him. Furious shades crowded at him, pushed at his nostrils, stung deep into his skin. He stood facing the void, rubbed their black filth off his flesh, spat them out of his mouth, wiped his eyes clean. He smashed at them, but they surged back. "Away!" he cried. He gathered his strength until his breath came like fire. "Away from me!" he ordered them. "Away! I am not dead flesh."

He struck at them, but they returned – now in the shape of huge, flapping vultures, tearing at his hair and clothing. "Away! I am not carrion for your maws!" He rained blows with his fists, exulted in the sound of them being crushed. He felt fierce in their dying.

They lay about him, choking in their spleen. He wielded the strength of the archangel; beside him fought every man who had ever walked upright. He cut his way into the heart of the darkness.

There he stood, on the brink, the black void open before him. The quest had ended; the search finished. The voice huddled before him. Richard waited, uncertain of what to do next. Gradually he became aware of an unexpected feeling. He found he no longer loathed this voice. For some inexplicable reason, he cared for this sickening heap lying before him. This voice that twisted the truth was part of him. He had brought it into the light, out of the filth and waste where he had banished it from sight. Suddenly, revelation struck him.

Was this why he had come? Was this the task Michaal had asked of him? He waited. Before his eyes, his voice began to take shape. Out of the shadows at his feet it took flesh: head twisted; body putrid, leprous; eyes defiant.

Here before him stood his brother, his twin, his other half: himself. His words went forth like the touch of a hand. "Iscariot. We have come now unto ending." The eyes, blank mirrors, returned his gaze, unknowing, sullen. "It is I. I am not dead, but have come back unto you, as I told you that I would." The eyes looked back, unblinking; they could not see beyond their own despair. They showed only bitterness, defiance.

"I have come back to you." The being talked gently, and around it glowed a soft radiance. He searched the face, trying to find the weakness, waiting for the lies.

It spoke again. "Come. We will return together."

Then it dawned on him: he had become the voice. It was he who stood defiant, he who stood unmoving, mute. It was his arms that hung lifeless at his sides; his tongue that stuck in his mouth – his own eyes that stared back, cold, unblinking.

"Do not think I loathe you." The radiant being came closer. "You are my kin, my brother. Wholeness cannot come to us without your free consent. You have knowledge of the darkness, I of the light. Let us cleave unto each other and be again as one. The time has come. All is past, forgiven."

Writhing anger surged through him, and underneath it, an even more terrifying feeling – anguished joy. Was he hearing the truth? Could such love be real? The hands reached toward him. He feared this embrace more than he had ever feared anything in all eternity. Could he let go of the horror, let go of the loneliness? He began to tremble. In this light, he saw with clarity all he had ever betrayed. The guilt choked him. He wanted to hide, but he found himself held by the gentleness in the other's eyes.

"There is no judgment, no need for guilt." The words entered his being like a sword of love. And as if in answer, a massive malevolence began to gather within him. A living presence, it sat up on its haunches within his being. He had become uttermost evil.

Flickering darkness gazed pridefully out through his unblinking eyes. Then, in that instant, Richard understood his destiny. He had come through eons, over lifetimes beyond count to stand, evil incarnate, before the angel of light. But he still had his own free will. This, he suddenly realized, was his moment of greatness. His destiny was to choose.

Richard felt guilt in his groins, Lucifer's thick pride in his throat, despair tightening in the sinews of his body. He who was man had taken to himself the full chalice of evil. He knew the depth of its horror. He, mankind, knew too well the price of pride. He had indeed earned in full the right to speak its fate. Richard saw now the awesome trust that had been put into his hands. He was human, weak and frail, filled with evil, but free to choose. The cosmos waited on his word.

His lips moved thickly, heavily, remaining mute. His tongue remained gagged. He willed his arms upward, willed them to reach out. He would embrace the light. He felt his eyes widen with a fear born of a longing he had known since time began, a longing so great he dared not speak the words.

"Help me," he cried out with his eyes. "Hold me!"

Richard felt himself taken in an embrace so loving that every atom of his being moved beyond itself in ecstasy. He had done the deed. Nothing would ever be the same again.

Chapter Thirteen

Pamela awoke to feel the ground beneath her shaking, to hear the sound of chasms closing, crevices shutting, water welling upward. She sat up. She felt a pushing within her. Then an urgent pressure. "Jamie!" Her voice was loud, plaintive. "Maia! The water's broken!"

Maia kissed her. "Hail, woman. Blessed is the fruit of thy womb. Let us help you now in this the time of our deliverance. Fisherman, fetch the water."

"It hurts," Pamela said. And indeed, though she could feel the child pushing down, something felt caught. A pressure was building. "Maia," she called. But Maia had run to fetch Jamie.

Pamela tried to breathe, but it didn't help. The constriction worsened. But what felt squeezed was not merely her abdomen, but her whole body. Her back felt twisted, taut; even her heart felt tight. She sat weakly on the edge of her bed. The child was too big, too monstrous to pass. Her memory of splitting like a beetle rose to mind.

She began to panic. She tried to call out, but her voice was too weak to carry far. All her energy was directed to enduring the waves of pain that were threatening to engulf her. Another spasm worse than the rest hit her, and she fell unconscious into nightmare. Like a beetle, she felt herself about to split in two. She wanted to cry out but found herself gagging. She thought she heard Maia calling out to her. She tried to open her eyes, but a hand reached up in the darkness and pulled her down into the underworld.

Frantically, she fought back, but she was caught tight in the grip of another who slowly, inexorably, drew her down, further and further, into a dark pit. Gradually, the darkness thinned to a dull gray, and before her, wrapped in swaddling clothing, was the child of her womb – the leper child.

The stench was overwhelming; its misshapen form revolted her. "No!" She pulled back from what she was being asked. "Let it die." This was asking too much.

Suddenly she was aware of Maia's voice shouting at Jamie. "The child's breaching. It will be stillborn. O'Ryan...do something. Orion, we need help. She can't do it alone. Oh, heaven help us now, at this, the moment of our deliverance."

Pamela gazed again at the malformed child, saw again its misshapen face, its beseeching eyes. She could not embrace it. To love such a child was beyond the possible. Firmly now, she stilled the panic in her heart.

A sense came to her that she was no longer alone. She felt a presence encircle her, waiting – a being, more herself than she was. Then Delana suffused her and she knew with full consciousness what was being asked of her: to embrace the uttermost horror of mankind, the ugliness, the sickness, the fear. Nothing could be left out. She had to embrace it all.

The leper child reached up its arms. How could she say no? She stepped forward and took the child into her arms. She smoothed its eyelids and then kissed it full on the lips. She cradled and rocked it, the tears running down her face. When she looked down at the face of her child again, she saw with clear eyes the most beautiful infant in the world.

Pamela awoke to Maia shouting in her ear. "It's coming. Now push. Breathe. Push."

She held tight to Maia's hands, pushed down with all her might. She groaned, pushed harder, felt its head, its shoulder, then its body slip free. A child's cry pierced her heart, burst it with joy. She lifted up her firstborn.
"My child. My love." Drawing the child close to her heart, she lay back, closed her eyes and drifted into that other world.

There before her was Richard, standing in sunlight, his blue eyes sparkling. Her heart leaped with love. She came forward and showed him their child. Gently he took the child into his arms.

Soul to soul, woman to man, man to woman, they met. It was as if they were once again in the garden, but now they faced each other in the knowledge of their own worth. Now beyond innocence, full with experience, they stood before each other in their maturity.

"The time before," Richard said, "I could not truly love you, for I asked from you what you could not give me – myself."

"The time before," Pamela said, "I could not truly love

194

you, for I was angry and weak."

She waited for him to speak. He looked across at her, saw her open face, her gentle eyes, felt a stirring within himself, a longing for her touch. She saw the need on his face, knew the beauty of his soul. "Freely, with all my heart do I love you, gentle man."

"And I, you."

They took each other's hand, the child cradled between them, and listened as the Supreme Logos spoke to them.

"Within each person on earth have I entered, awaiting this moment. You who are but the first of many, do I anoint with the power to make all things new.

"Woman, your time is upon you. Your innermost mystery will unfold like the petals of the rose, your touch will be as balm, your embrace will hold sway over all that is to come. You shall hold the sceptre of the new age."

"Man, without armor, without shield, without sword, you will walk the earth, welcomed by all. You shall be my waterbearer.

"This day do I enter with you, man and woman, into a new covenant. The child given unto you this day is the flesh of my promise and the vessel of this covenant that will dwell from this day on between us. For I shall dwell within you and within your children, and within your children's children for all the days of life to come."

The voice became larger, choruslike, as if untold numbers were united with it. "Uplift the heart in joy and laughter; we join with you in this greatest of celebrations."

A wordless peace fell over them, one that reached beyond even joy.

Mel arrived back in Centrex and stood panting before the LOMB doors. He pounded his fists against the heavy plasto-lax portals, but they stood mute and unmoving. Finally he stopped and simply stood there, panting, waiting.

Eventually, as if in their own good time, the LOMB doors rolled open. Hornepayne stood in the entrance, looking as if he were expecting him. "Come in."

"Is he here?"

"Come in. You look like you've been on a long journey."

"Has he returned?"

Hornepayne turned and gestured for Mel to follow. He led him into an anteroom off the main entrance. The room was small and furnished with monkish simplicity.

"Sit down. Catch your breath. You look as if you've just returned from the ends of the earth."

Mel nodded and sank into a chair.

"You look exhausted. Let me get you something." Hornepayne opened a cupboard and took down two ancient, glazed mugs.

Mel remembered those mugs – they'd once belonged to Pamela. He wondered what part she had played in all of this. He gripped the steaming mug and looked into the old man's patient gray eyes. "Can I tell you?" he asked.

Hornepayne nodded.

"I didn't mean it – not really. It just happened. No," he corrected himself. "That's a lie. I did mean it, actually. I..."

"Why don't you start at the beginning?" Hornepayne suggested.

Mel took a cautious sip. "You know I left Centrex early in the new year?"

Hornepayne nodded.

"I told them I needed a holiday. I hopped a transport to Europe. Things weren't the way you see them through your scanner. The alliance was falling apart. The work programs, the enclaves, Centrex control – people paid lip service but nothing more.

"Then one night I dreamed that Richard was at the foot of my bed. He had it all, someplace where I couldn't get to him. Here I was – nowhere – and Richard...Well, I woke up the next morning in a fury. I mean, I still had status, power. I could go anywhere." Mel paused, then corrected himself. "No, that's another lie.

"But at that moment my life gained purpose," Mel went on. "I decided at that moment I would find him."

"And?"

"Kill him! I was filled with hatred. I managed to slip away alone into the mountains, the lone hunter. I would find him, I resolved. I'd stop him from tormenting me...."

The half smile on Hornepayne's face seemed to distract the younger man. "I don't know," Mel said, looking uncomfortable. "I must have been suffering from hallucinogens – it's the only explanation for it all. But what happened in the mountains was so strange.

"I had hidden myself in a cave for the night, but just as the sun was coming up, I saw Richard silhouetted in the entrance. He didn't speak, he just walked toward me. And you know what? He put his arms around me." Mel looked over at Hornepayne. "He put his arms around me...after all I'd done to him."

"What did you do that was so horrible, Meldor?"

"I broke his vessels. I smashed them to pieces. On New Year's Eve, in his inner room – it was like his temple – I broke open the lock and went in and smashed everything inside to pieces. Didn't you know? I thought Pamela had told you."

"And why did you do such a thing?"

"He came over one night. We argued. He saw me for what I really was. He was getting too close. Maybe in truth I didn't even have a reason, maybe it was just spite. Back then, I think I wanted him to hate me. And what puzzles me even more – I thought I wanted to kill him. But that night in the cave, when he came up to me, I just let him hold me."

Hornepayne handed him a handkerchief. "It's okay, Mel. Cry. Maybe what you did was also necessary."

Mel remained deep in thought. Tears ran down his face. "Richard simply reached out and put his arms around me. Then he said, 'It's all over. Let's go home.'"

"I want to see Richard." His voice was that of a young boy's. "I want to see him in the flesh. To tell him I'm sorry." Sobbing choked his words. "I want to say let's forget the past. Let's start anew."

"And so you came back, hoping to find him here?"
"Yes."

The lights dimmed briefly and Mel looked startled.

Hornepayne spoke. "Centrex is losing its power. We'll be abandoning it soon. It's served its purpose."

"Things are changing in the outer world as well," said Mel

with a nod. "There's still chaos and confusion out there, but something has changed. Something has gone out of men's hearts. Some dark contagion has been lifted. There's still suffering, and there still isn't a lot of love, but as far as I can see, there's no longer that deep hatred of one man for another. Maybe it's just me." He looked over at Hornepayne. "I don't know anymore."

Before Hornepayne could answer, he began to talk again. "You know what I want to do with my life?" The tears streaked down his cheeks. "I've been thinking a lot about the holy city. I don't want to see Jerusalem destroyed. I want to go back to see that it doesn't happen." Then he paused and thought for a moment. "Wouldn't it be beautiful to turn the world into a sanctuary, a place filled with fruit and honey, and flowing with sweet, fresh water?"

Hornepayne held Mel's head in his lap and rocked him gently. "Yes, indeed," the old man said. "Things we never thought possible before can happen now."

Richard tossed in his sleep, wrapped in a timeless dream, where he saw himself rise to his feet, naked as a newborn child. The morning sun was burning off the mist. He lifted off from the earth. Upward he flew, until he was above the clouds. He flew higher and higher as the day faded into evening and the stars came toward him. Upward he flew, deeper into his Icarus dream, reaching for what he now knew was possible.

He was in the heavens in full transport beyond space and time, a pulsar of light, a dragon, flaming red, charging into the sun, only to find himself the reflected image of the solar light. Laughing aloud, he reached out to the seven-star dipper, took its handle and poured the riches of the heavens down upon the earth. He laughed again in pure delight at the triumph of this whole impossible dream.

The earth shone below him, an exquisite blue pearl in the universe, so fragile, so beautiful. A longing filled him to return to the security of space and time. He longed for the embrace of flesh and blood. It was time for the dream to end. Time to awake. He called out her name.

Pam looked up from putting leftovers from last night's party into the Fun Galore carry box. Though the traffic was noisy, she thought she'd heard Richard calling, very far off. Suddenly, she realized how much she missed him. She spoke aloud to the empty room: "Richard, I love you".

The words had been spoken, the tide was running full. Beacon to the sailor long at sea, she guided him home. Richard held her face in his mind's eye, opened to her love, which bridged both worlds. He let himself fall into that harmony, toward that figure that stood on the far shore, transporting back into present time and place. Just before he turned the doorknob, a voice spoke in his inner ear: "Now things we never thought possible before can happen."